CH Cl²

FLEUR DE CORSE

Catrin confronts a man trespassing on her Aunt Hazel's land, only to learn that he is Hazel's godson, Alex. He's a successful architect, handsome but irritating — and when he offers to buy Hazel's property, Catrin is immediately suspicious. Can she trust his motives, or does he have something to gain from the arrangement? Accompanying Hazel on a trip to Corsica, Catrin ponders this — but when Alex turns up unexpectedly, her feelings begin to change. Still, she's determined to uncover his true intentions for her aunt's land . . .

WENDY KREMER

FLEUR DE CORSE

LINFORD
Leicester

First published in Great Britain in 2018

First Linford Edition
published 2020

A catalogue record for this book is available
from the British Library.

ISBN 978–1–4448–4398–9

Published by
F. A. Thorpe (Publishing)
Anstey, Leicestershire

Set by Words & Graphics Ltd.
Anstey, Leicestershire
Printed and bound in Great Britain by
T. J. International Ltd., Padstow, Cornwall

This book is printed on acid-free paper

Confrontation

'Do you realise this is private property?' Catrin demanded. She stood defiantly and looked up at the stranger with heightened colour.

He was silent, and his dark eyes examined her closely. His tanned skin and rugged features suggested he came from an exotic background, but that impression died when he spoke. His accent was decidedly English without any unfamiliar nuances. There was a hint of amusement in his expression, and he didn't hesitate.

'This is a public pathway, so I'm not breaking the law.'

'Where you're now standing and where you came from is not the public pathway.'

Catrin wasn't sure about the rules and regulations but she hoped she sounded as if she did. There was a

1

public pathway through the field but it meandered along one of the sides. She remained focused, although she had a niggling feeling she would have been better off if she'd ignored him.

She was on her way to the village when she saw his long-limbed body climb through a gap where winds and storms had done some damage to the wall. Aunt Hazel couldn't afford professional repairs. Catrin decided she would come back later, and try to patch it up. She took a deep breath and hoped she sounded authoritative.

'The public pathway is through the kissing gate, in the corner. It goes along the hedge. You should use that. Scrabbling through a damaged wall only makes more damage.'

He brushed at his coat absentmindedly and attempted to look apologetic.

'Mea culpa!' he uttered, with a sweeping gesture. 'Someone has dumped logs across the road, so I couldn't park further down. I saw the gap and took the shortcut. If I'd known you were in charge of the kissing gate, I'd have climbed over the logs to test it with you.' He looked like he was enjoying himself.

'You don't need to kiss someone to use a kissing gate,' Catrin retorted hotly. 'I expect you know that very well!'

His eyes twinkled and he sighed exaggeratedly.

'More's the pity! Are you the owner of this hallowed ground?'

Annoyed, she shifted uneasily and brushed her windswept hair out of her face.

'No, but my aunt is,' she replied, 'and she'd tell you exactly what I'm telling you.'

'Ah! Then in that case, if you are not the owner, you have no right to whinge about anything. As I don't intend to wait until you fetch your aunt, and as there's no way you can stop me physically, I suggest you carry on, and so will I.'

Catrin's expression displayed her

growing annoyance. What an insufferable man, but she was too unsure of her legal rights to argue with him any more.

Noticing that he had silenced her and won, he saluted with a finger to his temple and moved off down the slope.

Catrin remained where she was for a moment and watched his tall figure striding confidently down towards the main road. The wind was playing with the folds of his soft coat and ruffling his hair. One thing was sure — he wasn't an ordinary rambler. He was too well dressed to be out on a walking tour. He was probably one of those odious types who were determined to win each and every argument, by fair means or foul.

She turned away, trying to forget their meeting, and inhaled the fresh aroma of the sunned grasses and flora. Spring had arrived. The last couple of days had been very sunny and the field was a mass of bright yellow dandelions and buttercups. The flowers moved their heads in waves as the soft breezes traversed the field.

Making her way to the gate, she paused and looked back. He was already through the bottom gate and she followed his tall figure as he strode down the road on the other side of the hedge.

She shrugged and vowed to check the rights and regulations about public pathways later on. She set off along the high-banked road leading to the village.

She heard pigeons making cooing sounds in the nearby wood. Glancing back along the road, she could see the pile of logs strewn across the surface, and beyond them, a car parked on the side. Someone with a tractor and trailer was coming from the village and its throaty knocking sound was unmistakable. It looked like the driver was on his way to collect the logs, so the stranger had told her the truth about why he'd used the gap in the wall.

A few minutes later, she reached the village. A handful of old cottages with slate roofs were dotted between houses that were more modern in style. They all sprawled along the road next to one another amidst neatly tended gardens. She loved the place and looked around in a moment of nostalgia.

Every time she came to visit Hazel, time seemed to stand still. Everyone knew everyone else here. Catrin stuck her hands into her pockets, passed the village school, the vicarage, the one-pump petrol station-cum-repair garage, the village hall and the police station, and finally reached the shop. It catered to the basic needs of the community, and it was their local post office, too.

Catrin wondered how long the Watsons could keep going. She couldn't remember anyone else ever serving behind the old-fashioned wooden counter. Hazel had mentioned that the Watsons were trying to find replacements to take over, but were unsuccessful so far. It would be a sorry day for the village and the surrounding farms if the shop closed down.

The old-fashioned bell above the

door tinkled as she went inside. The woman behind the counter looked up and smiled. She was busy replenishing packets of cigarettes on the shelf behind her.

'Hello, my dear. Visiting Hazel again? How are things with you?'

'Fine, thanks, Mrs Watson. You?'

'Yes, can't complain. Tom's rheumatism plays him up now and then, but he soldiers on. What can I get you?'

A few minutes later, Catrin strolled back to her aunt's again with a fresh loaf of bread and a carton of badly needed long-lasting milk.

She unzipped her jacket. Although the sun would disappear soon, the air was still pleasantly warm and very pure. She meandered back along the silent lane, through the stile, and down along the edge of the field. Last year's bracken lay dormant in the bordering hedge. Feathery green shoots of fern would soon emerge and cover the brown gaps.

Hazel's cottage was a converted

farmhouse that had been in her family for generations. The remaining farm-land now consisted of two fields rented out to a neighbouring farmer, the hilly field behind the house and a small ragged wood.

She hurried and hoped she wouldn't meet the stranger for a second time.

Reaching the house, she walked up the crazy stonework path. Ivy was growing rampant on the old brickwork and the garden was full of flowers. The road outside carried little traffic.

There was a modern bypass not far away, so drivers using this stretch of road were mostly people who lived locally. The fact that it wasn't busy also meant the next bus stop was several hundred yards away in the opposite direction.

The cottage was lonely, even if the village was only a stone's throw away across the field.

Hazel hadn't ever complained but Catrin began to wonder how she'd manage in the future.

'Hazel, I'm back, mission completed,' she called, as she hung her jacket upon the hall stand.

She hurried to the sitting-room and her smile faded when she saw Hazel's visitor.

Too Good to Be True

The man from the field was sitting comfortably in one of the armchairs, looking completely at ease. His dark eyes twinkled. He wore a suit that no provincial tailor had fashioned, with a sparkling white shirt and gold cuff links.

Hazel Aston was a pleasant looking woman in late middle age, somewhat plump, with pale blue eyes and curly greying hair. She looked up and smiled.

'Ah! Here's Catrin. We'll have milk for our tea after all.'

Catrin looked at her expectantly.

'Catrin, this is Alex. Alex has been visiting me almost since he was old enough to walk. His parents used to live in the village. It's a wonder that you haven't met before, but when you were here, he wasn't, and vice versa.'

Catrin nodded. He clearly hadn't

mentioned their meeting to Hazel or she'd have commented on it. Catrin was annoyed. It meant that with certainty, he already knew about the public pathway. Why hadn't he explained instead of making her feel foolish? She looked down at the carpet, gathered her thoughts, and then looked up at him boldly.

His face was ruggedly handsome. His mouth curled into a polite smile.

'Hello, Catrin!'

She dipped her chin.

'Hello!'

Hazel would have made fun of her, if she knew Catrin had told this man what to do.

'I'll just put some milk in a jug,' she said, wanting a moment to adjust. 'I'll be right back!'

She hurried down the corridor towards the kitchen. Looking for a suitable jug, she wondered why he made her nervous. She was normally confident of her abilities and didn't let things ruffle her easily. She decided it had to do with his manner, and perhaps because he knew he was attractive to women!

She felt more relaxed when she returned to the sitting-room. The sun skimmed the edges of the chintz curtain framing the open window. They suited the charm of the low-beamed room. The day was ending and the fabric shivered in the late afternoon breezes.

The armchairs had worn covers, the floral wallpaper was faded, and the surfaces of the well-polished furniture mirrored Hazel's life in the form of pictures, knick-knacks and personal memoirs.

Alex was a big man but he'd managed to fold himself into his chair and look at ease. One hand rested on his knee and the other on the armrest.

Catrin put the jug on the tray and sat down.

Aunt Hazel gestured towards him.

'I've mentioned my godchild Alex often, haven't I? He always pops in to see me whenever he's in the area.'

Catrin nodded. She recalled the name but she hadn't paid close attention because Hazel had three godchildren. The name Alex cropped up occasionally but they'd never met. She dug deep in her memories and recalled that Hazel had once mentioned he'd passed at a prestigious university.

Without commenting, Catrin helped herself to a cup of tea.

Hazel looked at Alex.

'Catrin is my niece,' she explained. 'She's my brother's daughter. I told you about Colin dying unexpectedly a couple of years ago, didn't I? It's strange that you two haven't met before, isn't it? Catrin always stays overnight when she comes.'

'Does she? That must be nice.' He looked at Catrin and his teeth flashed white in his tanned face as he regarded the attractive woman with a slim waist and shapely hips. At present, her almond-shaped eyes were sparkling with annoyance.

Catrin hesitated and was tempted to mention their meeting in the field after all, just to provoke him, but Hazel would think it strange they hadn't mentioned it earlier. Her sense of fairness won over, and she decided not to bother.

Just because he enjoyed poking fun didn't mean the man was a monster. Someone who visited Hazel regularly couldn't be that bad. She'd probably never meet him again.

She decided to be polite and avoid any confrontation. She took a sip of tea.

'What do you do, Alex?' she asked. 'Hazel may have mentioned it, but I can't remember.'

'I'm an architect.'

Catrin viewed him and decided if appearances were anything to go by, he must be doing well.

'That must be an interesting job.'

An architect would know all about public pathways, and probably knew more about the topography of the village and its surroundings than she did. That fact didn't particularly endear him to her at present.

His brows lifted and the corners of his mouth turned up. He could read her expression.

'Yes, it is.' He put his cup back down on the table.

'Alex is very successful,' Hazel added.

He smiled at Hazel.

'I'm still climbing. It's a shark's business.'

'But you are making a name for yourself. Last time you were here you mentioned you'd won a commission to redesign a house on Corsica for a French businessman.' Hazel turned to Catrin. 'Alex's grandfather came from Corsica, so his personal connection to the island has helped him win a couple of jobs there.'

He met Catrin's questioning eyes. He laughed softly.

'True. The right connections are always helpful. It's much harder to get a foothold in the UK, though. Most newly qualified architects end up as part of a team. A good team, if they're lucky. If not, they end up as a dogsbody for years on end. I was lucky enough always to work independently.'

'So you build exclusive holiday homes for people with too much money,' Catrin commented, with a hint of acidity.

His brows lifted.

'Everyone needs money to build a house, whether they're rich or not.' He shrugged. 'Sometimes my client is affluent, sometimes not. My designs are not always exclusive. Ordinary people need homes, too, and I try hard to give them the best possible result. Sometimes I can persuade a prospective buyer to convert instead of building from scratch.

'I also like Corsica too much to want to see it full of dazzling white cubes that stand out like eyesores. I put forward ideas to suit them and the surroundings. Most of the time people fall in line with my suggestions, but not always.' He changed the direction of the conversation. 'And what do you do?'

She took a hasty sip of tea.

'I'm an assistant curator in a museum.'

He nodded.

'Oh, yes. I remember Hazel telling me that. I expect it suits you down to the ground — looking after old objects in the hallowed surroundings of a museum. No competition, no pressure, no rivalry, and no struggles to make a profit.'

Catrin knew it was tit-for-tat.

'You clearly have no idea about the competition between museums, or about the never-ending struggle to remain financially viable. We're often on the edge of disaster.'

Hazel intervened, no doubt wondering why they were beginning to sound like squabbling small children.

'It's a pity I didn't know you were coming, Alex. I'd have made a cake.'

'Your cake is mouth-watering, but that's not why I come, as you well know.'

Hazel turned to Catrin.

'We were just talking about how I'll manage to cope financially in old age. Alex has made me a very kind offer.'

Catrin did a double take. She was immediately suspicious.

'An offer? What offer?'

'He said he'd buy the cottage and the fields and I can stay here as long as I live. It would provide me with enough money to be very comfortable for the rest of my life.'

Catrin bristled. Noticing her expression, he butted in.

'It's only a suggestion,' he hastened to say. 'Hazel will need time to think about it.'

'What would you do with it? The land, I mean?'

He shrugged.

'I don't know yet. It was a spontaneous suggestion. The wood might be under some kind of protection order. You said you rented the fields out to Billy Rainer, Hazel?'

'Yes. He uses them for grazing and

18

making hay. He doesn't do much with the one behind the house because it is on the slope and therefore more troublesome. He puts the cows there for weeks at a time in the good weather, but then it's harder for him when it comes to milking time.'

Catrin wondered if Alex already had planning permission to build on the field. She wouldn't put it past him to cut down all the trees in the small copse either. If he'd grown up locally, he probably had the right connections everywhere. Architects were interested in making money, and not playing social benefactors. Perhaps he was planning to build houses there.

She managed to keep her mouth shut. It was not her concern, but she intended to discuss it with Hazel when he wasn't around.

They chatted about generalities and the village. He still knew many of the villagers, even though he'd moved to London. Hazel asked what he was doing at present and he told her about a bungalow on the French coast.

'My client is a politician who lives in Paris most of the time. He wants a holiday home and bought the land some years ago. Apparently, there was a tussle until the local authorities awarded planning permission, but that's settled and I can go ahead.

'I presume he wants to impress fellow politicians. His wife comes from a very wealthy family, and I get the impression that financially the sky's the limit. That's ideal for me and a fantastic opportunity.'

'How did you get the commission?' Hazel asked. 'Did someone recommend you?'

'No. He saw something I built on Corsica while he was visiting a friend. He got in touch. I visited the site, discussed the possibilities, and made some rough sketches. He liked my ideas, and I was in.'

'It sounds easy, but I don't suppose it was.'

'No, it wasn't. I hope it will generate

other work. He belongs to affluent circles, and in my business recommendation goes a long way.'

'Do you build ordinary houses?' Catrin asked.

He smiled crookedly.

'Yes, of course. I just told you so. I always will. Sometimes the challenge of redesigning an older house or building a practical home for a modern family gives me almost as much pleasure as creating something exclusive and very expensive.'

Catrin didn't say what she thought. A rich client would bring him larger financial gains than building or redesigning something for an average family. She reached for her cup and took another sip.

Hazel beamed at them.

'I'm really proud of you both. You've both achieved something special. I sometimes wondered if university demands would smother your ambitions, but they didn't, and you are both still young. Who knows what's still ahead.'

Alex stood up.

'Well, I'd better be going. I've promised to call on my sister on the way back to London before flying back to France early tomorrow morning.' He went across and bent down to kiss Hazel on her cheek. 'I'll see you next time I'm in the area. Think about my offer. I have some spare assets at present. I did think about buying more land on Corsica, but if I bought your fields it would be a solid investment, too, and give you security for the future.'

Hazel smiled at him.

'Thanks for calling and I hope to see you again soon. If you give me some warning, I guarantee some cake next time.'

He turned in Catrin's direction.

'Bye, Catrin. Don't get lost amongst all the grime and antiquities.'

She smiled stiffly.

'I won't, and I hope none of your buildings collapse around your feet in a cloud of dust.'

He grinned and left the room in a flurry of action. He put on his coat in the hall and Catrin remained silent until she heard the front door close.

A Helping Hand

Catrin didn't want to broach the subject too soon, but she was still worried about Alex's offer. Later, when they were preparing the evening meal, she turned to her aunt.

'You're worried about money?' she asked casually.

Hazel laughed softly.

'I've worried about it ever since your uncle died. My widow's pension isn't much and I'm too old to find a decent job. I thought about doing so after Ken died but it's too far to town. How would I get there and back? There's no regular bus service and I'd have to walk at least two miles every day to and from the bus stop — summer and winter.

'I'm careful about what I spend. I grow most of my vegetables, and with Billy's rent for the fields I manage to cope with rates, water, electricity, and all the rest. I manage. Other people are worse off than I am.'

Catrin was remorseful. She knew Hazel didn't have much money, but she'd never given it much thought. She brought a bag of groceries whenever she came and Hazel had never complained about her situation.

'Why didn't you mention you'd like a job, but transport was a problem? You have a driving licence and we could have found a good second-hand car.'

'And where would I find the money for that?'

'I would have helped or I expect the bank would have given you a loan.'

Hazel was peeling some potatoes. She shook the water from her hands, looked at Catrin and smiled.

'That's why I never mentioned it. I have all I need. I just need to watch where the money goes, just like millions of other people. I know you already help your mum out if she needs something special — she told me so. It's enough that you still visit me whenever you have the time. You're almost the daughter I never had.

'Don't worry; I'm fine. I'll give Alex's offer some thought. It is not as though I should hang on to the ground because there's someone in the family who intends to be a farmer, is it?'

Catrin didn't look up.

'After hearing Alex's offer, I wonder about his motives, that's all,' she said. 'Perhaps he has plans that he hasn't told you about?'

Hazel looked at her with a surprised expression.

'He hasn't got any plans. He only offered after I mentioned money was short. I expect he recalled how his grandfather on his mother's side came to the UK to give his family a better life and worked like a demon to achieve that aim. I bet money was short for them, too.'

She dropped the potatoes into the pot to boil.

'Alex's father took over the business

when his own father died — a small building company. I think that's when Alex's interest in building began. Alex began helping in the firm in his spare time when he was growing up and his parents bought a cottage in the village. They lived there until Anthony retired to Corsica with Maria. I got to know them all well and they asked me to be Alex's godmother.

'Alex used to pass here on his way to grammar school and I often dragged him inside in winter to warm him up. Sometimes his dad could take him or fetch him, but most of the time he had to catch the bus.

'I get birthday and Christmas cards from all of them, and Anthony and Maria keep inviting me to visit them. By the time his father retired from the business, Alex was a qualified architect. He kept the business going for local work. They're a close family.'

Catrin nodded.

'I can't remember them, but I didn't start coming to visit you regularly until after university. Perhaps they'd left by then.'

'They had that pretty cottage on the end of the row, and Anthony built a lovely extension at the back.'

'It seems strange to me that Alex is prepared to buy your land if he doesn't have plans for it. You could build houses yourself, sell them, and make a profit, even though you'd have to employ someone to build them for you. He could shortcut all that, and make a bigger profit.'

Hazel laughed.

'Oh, Catrin! I'm sure he isn't using some dubious strategy to trick me into something I'll regret later. He's not like that. He only made the offer today because I mentioned I was thinking of paying someone to dig the garden this autumn and had to scrape the money together to do so. I've always managed to do it myself but it's tough going nowadays.'

She shrugged.

'It was just a normal conversation,

and he made his offer spontaneously because he wanted to help.'

Catrin let the subject drop. She decided to check things out, and find out if there was any protection order on the wood, or if anyone had submitted building plans for the area.

After their evening meal Hazel wanted to watch one of the soaps on the TV, so Catrin decided to do something about the gap in the wall.

She borrowed a pair of Hazel's gardening gloves. Two hours later, she was tired.

It was much more difficult than she imagined. Building a wall with only rough stones and no cement took skill. You needed a good eye to guess which stones fitted together well. They had to knit in a way that was stable, and provide stability for the next layer.

She filled any apertures with chippings and grit as she went along. The light was fading fast when she slapped her hands together and stood back, satisfied with her efforts. The result wasn't perfect, but she had closed some of the gap.

She'd try to do some more before she left on Sunday and hope it would hold.

On Saturdays, she normally drove Hazel into town to give her a chance to stock up on bulky goods. Noting the state of Hazel's gloves, she now needed to buy at least one pair of new gloves.

She went down the field towards the cottage. Hazel had lit the fire and there was smoke curling out of the chimney. Catrin glanced into the distance. There was the golden light of the late afternoon everywhere and she watched wild pigeons flying in and out of the nearby wood, cooing as they did so.

Slipping out of her boots outside the kitchen door, she joined Hazel in the sitting-room. There was a smell of apple coming from the wood burning in the fireplace.

She looked at the TV.

'Was it a good episode?'

'I do wish the two main characters would sort it out. I keep waiting for them to admit they love each other.'

'Ah! You and thousands of others. That's what keeps the programme going.'

Hazel laughed.

'And did you manage to do anything? Sid Fellows used to keep the walls in shape for me, but he's getting on for ninety and he can't any more.'

Catrin nodded.

'I've made a start. I'll do a bit more tomorrow. Sid will probably throw up his hands in despair when he sees the results, but the main thing is that it's safe and won't fall over.'

'I'm surprised you even noticed it was damaged. It's right up in the far corner.'

Catrin didn't want to confess that Alex had come that way.

'Oh! Just a fluke. It looked different somehow and I checked. I hope I can do a lot more tomorrow.'

'You shouldn't be working when you come here.'

Catrin's eyes twinkled.

'I enjoy it. I'm indoors all week. Being out in the fresh air is lovely. I love it here. You never ask me to do anything. I volunteer because I hope it helps you in some way.'

Hazel nodded.

'Well, I'm grateful, whatever you do. Like tomorrow, when we go to town. If I had to cart heavy shopping back by bus, it would mean several trips to the supermarket. What about some cocoa?'

Hazel switched off the television and pushed herself up with help of the arms of the chair. She looked tired.

'You told me the doctor has prescribed tablets for blood pressure,' Catrin said. 'Have you taken them today?'

From the slightly flustered expression on Hazel's face, Catrin could tell she hadn't.

'Don't fuss, Catrin. I'm not even sure that they do any good. It doesn't seem to make much difference if I take them or not.'

'That's silly. The doctor doesn't

prescribe medication for fun. You ought to take them. Didn't he mention sending you to a specialist to do some tests? Did you go?'

'No. A fuss about nothing. I'm getting older. It's quite normal that I don't have the strength or the stamina to do things that I could twenty or thirty years ago.'

She began to walk towards the kitchen.

'That's true,' Catrin said, 'but if the doctor says the tablets will help you to cope longer and better, you should listen to him.'

Hazel waved her hand around as an answer, as she went through the door.

Catrin called after her.

'If you just take the tablets now and then, it won't do you much good. Would you like me to talk to him?'

Hazel popped her head around the framework again, and looked agitated.

'Don't you dare!'

Catrin lifted her hands in defence.

'All right! I won't, promise! But

please take them. I'm only telling you because I care.'

Hazel's expression softened.

'I know that, love. I don't take advice easily. When your uncle was alive, he kept me in line. I think I'm getting very stubborn in my old age, aren't I?'

Catrin laughed softly and covered the ground between them to give her a quick hug. She still had her arm round her aunt's shoulders when they reached the kitchen and they were both smiling. Catrin washed her hands as Hazel busied herself making them cocoa.

Catrin loved the compact old-fashioned kitchen with its huge farmhouse table, porcelain sink, and its dark green Aga. There was a jug of country flowers in the centre of the scrubbed table, and when she looked out of the window Catrin could see the garden. Springtime was already splashing bright colours everywhere.

She couldn't see them, but knew there were rows of various vegetables growing and prospering under Hazel's critical eye at the bottom of the garden.

They sat companionably. Hazel started to make a list of what she wanted to fetch tomorrow, and Catrin suggested additions while thinking about how she could persuade Hazel to take better care of herself.

★ ★ ★

Later, upstairs in what she almost considered as 'her' bedroom, she looked around at the pinewood furniture and the floral patterned wallpaper. Hazel's cottage was almost a second home, and whenever she had a spare weekend, she visited either Hazel or her mother.

Her mother was still very busy. She had a part-time job in a flower shop, and Catrin's brother and his wife and their baby son lived a short distance away. Her mother got on well with Catrin's sister-in-law, and she offered her baby-sitting services quite often.

Catrin missed her dad very much,

but she was trying hard to accept he wasn't around any more.

She leaned back and looked at the ceiling. The cottage was rather isolated and Hazel probably spent a lot of time on her own.

She had plenty of friends in the village, she knew heaps of other people, she took part in church events, and her gardening filled up an awful lot of her spare time, but she wouldn't always be so active.

Catrin picked up her book from the bedside table. She'd have to give the whole situation closer consideration.

Alex Lorenzi's proposal was unexpected. She didn't want Hazel to think she was interfering.

For the first time, Catrin also wondered how much longer Hazel could cope without help.

More Than Meets the Eye

Back at work the following Monday, she found out that a public footpath was open to the public at all times. She dug further and found there was a Country-side Act that provided subsidies for 'sensitive management' of the country-side for those people who opted into a special scheme. She wondered if that could be applicable to Hazel's wood-land.

She didn't feel completely at ease about making enquiries, but she per-suaded herself that it was exactly as if she was checking a project for the museum. They never organised a new exhibition without all the preliminary planning and checking. In the same way, she wanted to know exactly what someone could do with Hazel's land once he owned it.

Catrin met her friend Gloria for a

meal after work that evening. Amongst other things, Catrin told her about Hazel and that she was worried.

'And you think this man is after her money?'

'Not after her money. Hazel hasn't got any money! I'm wondering if this man is merely after the land at a knock-down price. He's an architect, and Hazel owns three fields and a small coppice. The wood is wild, because there's no-one to do the proper kind of work to keep it under control. It must be a haven for small animals.'

'And you think he wants to buy the land off her and build on it? Do you have any proof?'

Catrin shook her head.

'Nothing definite. I'm not sure if the planning authorities will give me any information if I ask.'

'I shouldn't think he'd apply for anything unless he actually owned the land, would he?'

'Perhaps not, but he could make tentative enquiries. It's probably quite normal for an architect to sidestep potential problems in advance. It'd be a waste of time and money to make plans unless he's sure he will get building permission. The ground could be contaminated in some way for all he knows.'

Gloria took a fork of salad and munched it.

'Is it?'

'Good heavens, no! It's been farming territory for centuries. The fields were part of a large estate once, but it was split up after the war, when the money ran out.'

'What's he like?'

'Attractive, in his thirties, confident, clever, and he seems to be well off.'

'He sounds like boyfriend material. Is he married, engaged, spoken for?'

Catrin coloured slightly. She could easily conjure such a clear picture of him in her mind, and it bothered her. She didn't want to admit how much he'd impressed her.

'I checked his business website.

There was no mention of a family. He did mention his sister when he left. His website is very professional and it shows he has designed some interesting looking houses and buildings. One of them, on Corsica, won an international prize.'

Gloria forked some more salad and declared.

'Grab him, Catrin! He sounds like a good catch. Once you've softened him up, he'll tell you what he intends to do with your aunt's land.'

Catrin tossed her head.

'I don't think you can 'soften him up'. He seems outwardly very relaxed, but his website shows me that he's very professional and single-minded. I think his work is very important to him.'

'I thought you said you don't know him?'

'I don't, but sometimes you get a feeling about someone, don't you? There's more than meets the eye in the person of Alex Lorenzi.'

'Stop tap-dancing around! Admit it

— you fancy him! Lorenzi? Is he Italian?'

'No, he's British but one of his grandfathers came from Corsica, and he still has strong ties to the island. Hazel said his parents went to live there after they retired.'

'And you think he's good-looking?'

'There's a photo of him on his website. Take a look. Tell me what you think. Just as long as he treats Hazel fairly and doesn't have plans that will turn her life upside down, I couldn't care less about him as a person, even if he is attractive.'

'He sounds luscious. Just remember that you don't really know if he has any plans for your aunt's fields. It's still all supposition on your part, isn't it? Perhaps you ought to give him the benefit of the doubt.'

'Perhaps, but I don't trust him.'

'Well, he sounds more exciting than your latest. What's his name? I've forgotten. You've been seeing a lot of each other, haven't you?'

'You mean Brian? It was never serious and I haven't see him for a couple of weeks. We don't have much in common. He liked partying and painting the town red every time we went out. I like having fun, but I need hassle-free, relaxing times, too.'

Later that week, Catrin phoned her mother. After the usual kind of preamble, her mother mentioned that Hazel had a bad chest, and wasn't being careful.

'I rang her the other day and she sounded terrible. She was croaking like a frog and coughing all the time. I told her to go to the doctor, but you know Hazel, I expect she won't listen. She insisted that lots of Vick and plenty of rest would do the trick. Phone her and try to talk some sense into her?'

'OK, I'll phone her later. How are things with you? Is everything all right?'

'I'm fine. I'm looking after the baby this weekend. David won tickets for a weekend in London, and asked if I could look after him.'

'And I expect you said no?' Catrin said, tongue-in-cheek.

'What do you think? I'm looking forward to it. He's such a sunny boy. He reminds me of David at the same age. He used to smile at everyone, too. You were always cautious with strangers. I asked Gaynor to give me Saturday off, so that I can concentrate on my grandson.'

'I can just imagine how it will go. Trips with the pram to all the places your cronies are likely to be, and using every opportunity to spoil him. Mum, remember that Jan will have trouble settling him down again if you spoil him rotten over the weekend.'

'Grandparents are supposed to spoil their grandchildren.' Her tone changed. 'I wish your dad was around. He'd be so proud of him. Just think! Two and a half days of him, all to myself!' she added, more cheerfully.

'Mum!'

Her mother chuckled on the other end of the line.

'I'm only joking. I'll try not to smother him with too much love. When are you coming home?'

'If you don't need me for anything special, I'll come in a week or two. Perhaps at the end of the month?'

'Well, don't forget. We can go on a shopping spree.'

'Perhaps. Take care, Mum.'

'Take care yourself, love, and remember to phone Hazel. Let me know how things go.'

'I will.'

★ ★ ★

After work that evening, Catrin was planning to ring Hazel but another phone call scotched that idea. She picked up the phone and was startled when she heard Alex Lorenzi's voice.

'Catrin? This is Alex. Am I interrupting something? Have you a moment to spare?'

She pulled herself together and hoped he didn't notice her surprise.

'Oh, Alex, how are you? No, you're not intruding. How can I help? How did you get my number?' she added as an afterthought.

There was amusement in his voice.

'I could have asked Hazel, but I didn't want to make her suspicious. It took me all of two minutes by using an internet telephone search.'

She cleared her voice.

'Oh . . . and how exactly can I help you?' Catrin was curious but she presumed he wasn't calling for a private reason. It probably had something to do with Hazel. If he believed she'd help him and encourage Hazel to sell him her fields, he was in for a surprise.

'It's about Hazel.'

'I thought it might be.'

He chuckled.

'I could have been phoning to find out if you'd come out with me.'

She coloured and was glad he couldn't see her. She didn't comment.

He then sounded more serious.

'Hazel's not well. I phoned her a

week back to ask for someone's address for Dad. She sounded awful. I was in the area today and went to see her. She has bronchitis or something worse and she won't listen to the doctor. She keeps pottering around in the garden, even though the weather has been rotten recently. She seems to think everything will go into decline if she doesn't do something every day.'

'She's always had the attitude that by doing a bit every day it is less work than an all-out attack every couple of weeks. Actually, my mother phoned me earlier today and she said she sounded bad. I was planning to phone her this evening . . . Do you often go out of your way to see Hazel?' Catrin was too curious not to ask.

'No, but my mother asks about her whenever I see her, and sends messages that I dare not forget to deliver. I like your aunt and I think she likes getting visitors because she has no direct family.'

'I'm a niece. That's fairly direct,'

Catrin said sharply.

'Yes, that's true. I wasn't intending to be rude. I just mean that she has no children of her own, so I think she loves regular visitors. I've called now and then ever since my grammar school days.'

There was nothing objectionable in what he said, so she remained silent.

He ploughed on.

'I couldn't persuade her to go to see the doctor, so I called at the surgery on my way home and asked him to pop in when he had a moment to spare. He seems to be a very nice chap, and even if he didn't go into the medical details about her state of health, he said it was typical of Hazel. He said she doesn't always follow his advice. He promised to call at the cottage and phone me back.

'He did, later that day, and said she had acute bronchitis. I asked if a change of air and a few weeks in the sun would help. He jumped at the idea.'

'Sounds sensible, but where do I

come into all of this?'

'She trusts you and you can convince her it's for her own good. I'm sure someone from the village will keep an eye on the cottage and the garden if she goes away. I phoned the people who lived next door to my parents and asked them if they'd do it, and they didn't hesitate to say yes.'

'Hazel can't afford a holiday and she won't take charity. My mum has asked her a couple of times to go with her on a coach trip and offered to share the cost, but Hazel wouldn't budge.'

'Ah, that's where I come into it. I'll offer her the use of my home on Corsica. That will cost her nothing, and I'll spin a story about having a free flight because I use the airlines so often.'

Startled, Catrin could only think how efficiently he was organising everything.

'Now that we've met, I thought it was a good idea to include you in the plot. That's why I'm phoning. Could you find time to take her there one weekend? Hazel has never been abroad on her own, has she? Travelling solo would frighten her and put her off going. You have a better chance of persuading her to go — especially if you promise to take her there and pick her up,' he added. 'I'll pay for your tickets, too. There are decent flights at a reasonable price if you book in advance.'

She was lost for words for a moment, then managed to reply.

'If she agreed, I can afford my own air ticket. I'm expecting a batch of items for an exhibition any day now but I could manage to fit it in at the weekend.'

'That sounds good. If you take her there Friday evening, and fly back on Sunday, it will give you time to settle her in the house. My parents live close by and they'll keep an eye on her once you've left. I thought a couple of weeks would make all the difference.'

He was steamrollering her and his words whizzed around her brain. She told herself to be sensible. If Hazel had bronchitis, some warm air and new surroundings would do her good.

'Why are you doing this?'

'Because I like her. I know this is all very sudden, but think about it.'

'OK, but I'll go to see Hazel before I agree to anything.'

'Good! I'll give you my number. I've already offered the house to Hazel. When she brings it up, you can see how she feels, and if you decide it would do her good, you can encourage her to accept my offer. I'll organise the flights.'

'If you do, I'll pay my own flight.'

'OK, OK! I understand that. The house is empty most of the time. I don't rent it out, so there's no problem about a suitable date. If you can persuade her, choose whatever suits you both best. I'd take her myself, but I'm up to my eyes in a project in France at present. I just haven't got the time.'

Catrin scrabbled around to find a piece of paper and a pen.

'Give me your number. I'll let you

know how things work out, and then we can go into more detail.'

Judging by their conversation, it didn't sound like there was a Mrs Alex Lorenzi.

Benefit of the Doubt

Later that evening Catrin was still puzzled. She told her friend Gloria about Alex's call.

'Wow! If he's going to that much trouble, he must care about your aunt. Not many people would offer to finance someone else's holiday. It's not as though he's a relative, is it?'

'Yes, that's what bothers me. What's his real motive?'

Gloria laughed.

'You are quite determined to cast him as the scoundrel in the plot. Have you considered that he just likes your aunt, and wants to help?'

Catrin shook her head.

'Perhaps you're right. I suppose I should give him the benefit of the doubt for Hazel's sake. It's not going to be easy to persuade her to go away. I know that already.'

'She's lucky that so many people are interested in her welfare. You're related, but lots of aunts have no contact at all with their nieces or nephews.'

'Hazel has always supported and helped me. It was sometimes easier to talk to her about things than to my mother. She helped me get over my first boyfriend when he dumped me. She made me see that there was no point in clinging to a man just for the sake of having a boyfriend and that it didn't matter if a woman ended up single these days. I always think of her as a friend, not just an aunt.'

Gloria nodded.

'Then concentrate on that, and think about what's best for her. Did you find out anything about planning permission for her fields or the immediate surroundings?'

'I've tried, but nothing definite so far. When I phoned, they gave me the number of another department. No-one seems directly responsible, or knows what I want to know. I'll see if I can have a couple of hours off to go there personally.'

'What about finding time to take your aunt to Corsica, if you can persuade her to go? It sounds quite glamorous. I thought you were busy at the museum preparing for that new exhibition in the autumn.'

'We are, but I expect I can get off earlier on Friday to take her to Corsica, and fly back on Sunday, but it will have to be soon otherwise the bronchitis will just get worse. He said his parents live close by, and that they'll keep an eye on her during her stay. Hazel is used to being on her own, so I think she'd manage well if they help her with shopping and check up on her from time to time.'

'Let me know how things work out.'
'Will do.'

* * *

When she called to see Hazel, Catrin could see that she was not well. She was pale, had dark rings under her eyes, and she coughed continually. She didn't mention Alex, or that she had seen the doctor.

Catrin pottered around the cottage, doing bits and pieces of work. That merely irritated Hazel, because they were jobs she usually did herself, but had neglected because she felt too weak.

Catrin left Hazel and went into town to do the shopping on her own. She couldn't remember when that had happened before. She began to worry that Hazel might end up with something more serious than bronchitis. Alex was right. She had to do something.

After she got back, she suggested they have an early supper, and could see relief on Hazel's face when Catrin suggested she went to bed straight after.

Catrin made them a supper of pasta with a cheese sauce, something Hazel usually enjoyed. She played around with it and ate little. Trying to pave the way for her suggestion about Corsica,

Catrin asked if there was any local news.

Hazel coughed for a few seconds before she drank some table water.

'Not a lot of news. The vicar announced another jumble sale with the aim of increasing the fund for restoring the church tower last Sunday.'

'You went to church?'

'I didn't feel so bad last week.' She straightened. 'You know the old saying — a week to come, a week to stay, and a week to go.'

Catrin didn't comment. It didn't look likely that Hazel's bronchitis would disappear unless something was done about it soon.

'Oh, the Watsons have help at the shop at the moment,' Hazel continued. 'A distant relative, a young woman with a little girl. She's trying it out during the school holidays, and if she likes the shop, she'll take it on permanently.'

'Oh, that's good. I've wondered a couple of times what will happen when the Watsons retire.'

'Yes, I hope that it works out. I haven't met her, but Alex told me about her. He went to the shop to get me some fresh milk when he was here.'

'Alex? He was here?' Catrin already knew that he'd called, but she had to approach the subject carefully. 'Did you know that Alex phoned me, and told me you are not feeling well?'

Hazel considered her carefully.

'Did he? There was no need for him to fuss.'

'He was worried, and to be honest, now that I'm here, so am I. You need a holiday. Some sun and a change of scenery. In fact, he told me his home on Corsica is empty at present.'

Hazel cut in more sharply on the conversation.

'I know that. And?'

'He thought, and I agree with him, that a holiday would do the trick.'

'I'm fine here. It'll go of its own accord, in the same way that it came.'

'But it'll go much faster if you can bask in the sun for a couple of weeks.'

Hazel's back was straight as a broomstick.

'I don't take charity, and I have no money to go gallivanting around the Continent.'

'It's not charity. Alex likes you and wants to help. He said the house was empty anyway. His parents live close by, and you wouldn't need to spend more than you do here.'

'And the air fare?'

'Ah! Apparently, Alex automatically collects points whenever he flies and when he's collected enough he gets a free flight. He said he'd give you his current free flight. It doesn't actually cost him anything, so you wouldn't need to feel beholden. You only need to pack a suitcase.'

Hazel was silent for a moment and eyed her carefully.

'The two of you have got it all worked out, haven't you? Who will keep an eye on the cottage? I've never flown, so how am I supposed to gallivant around the Continent without ending up in the wrong place? In fact, I haven't been on holiday since I went on that coach trip to Weston-Super-Mare with your parents, after your uncle died.'

Relieved that she hadn't rejected the idea outright, Catrin laughed.

'It's about time you did. You could ask someone you know in the village to keep an eye on the cottage, and I'll take you there. It will be my contribution to the scheme. Oh, come on, Hazel! It'll do you good.'

Hazel stood up.

'I'll leave the washing up to you.'

Catrin nodded impatiently.

'Of course. Promise to think about it?'

Hazel's tired face nodded.

'Yes, OK, I will. We'll talk again tomorrow.'

Perfect Place

It had been a rush, but they'd made it.

Hazel was excited and nervous about her first flight. Her excitement was infectious.

Catrin had forgotten how it felt when she'd flown for the first time. The cold air-conditioning in the plane didn't help Hazel's cough, but the steward supplied them with plenty of water to drink when Catrin explained that it helped.

Even though they were wearing lighter summer clothes, when they landed, they noticed a difference in temperature, even inside the airport building.

During his last phone call, Alex told her that his father would be there to meet them. There was a sparse line of people waiting near the barrier. Catrin looked for a sign with their names but

Hazel spotted him straightaway, and moved confidently in his direction.

'Anthony! How kind of you to meet us.'

He came towards them and hugged Hazel.

'It's good to see you, Hazel.' He was tallish with a square, sunburned face, and black eyes. His hair was thick and peppered with grey. He had a solid frame and his mouth stretched into a generous smile. He turned to Catrin.

'I'm sorry, you must be Catrin.' He held out his big hand. 'Alex told me you were coming with Hazel.'

Catrin shook hands and smiled.

'Yes, and you are Mr Lorenzi. Pleased to meet you.'

She was glad he was there. She suddenly realised Alex had given her no telephone number or address. What would she have done if he hadn't turned up?

'Welcome, both of you.' He motioned them along, grabbing the handle of Hazel's case and gesturing towards

Catrin's overnight bag. She shook her head and gripped it firmly. 'My car is outside.'

They followed him. The heat was heavy and the air seemed to shimmer. Catrin felt a prickling of sweat on her forehead and between her shoulder blades. The sky was a flawless blue and she inhaled the perfume of Corsica. It was a heady mixture of herbs and some kind of resinous additions.

His car was elderly, serviceable and, if looks were anything to go by, much used. Anthony Lorenzi explained there was no point in having a new car.

'We live inland, and as soon as you leave the main road, the roads and tracks are often demanding. Reliability and a four-wheel drive are more important features.'

Hazel was engrossed in studying the landscape as they sped along. The road grew steeper and it was running through an arid terrain. Thorny shrubs hedged the roadway. Mr Lorenzi explained they were roughly following a ridge of craggy mountains that ran the whole length of the island. There was little traffic and they left clouds of dust behind them marking their progress.

Catrin was glad of the breeze from the open window. It helped to cool her hot skin. From a distance, the lower areas of the mountainous ridges looked greener. She suddenly spotted the sea on the horizon between the hills. It was a brilliant blue.

They also passed vineyards, and Catrin wondered if it was her imagination that she could actually smell salt in the air. She saw the ocean more often now as the road twisted and turned on its approach to their destination.

Anthony pointed to a large group of buildings atop some steep cliffs on one side. Catrin couldn't see a road leading there, but undoubtedly, there must be one.

He explained over the sound of the engine.

'That is the nearest town to where we

live, and to Alex's place. You can get most things there, and of course, there is always fresh fish to be had down in the harbour.'

'Harbour?' Hazel queried. 'It looks like it is on top of the mountain.'

He laughed.

'That is the upper part of the town. There is an older, lower part, down below, out of sight from here.'

'Can I walk there from the house?'

He chuckled.

'Yes, but I wouldn't advise it unless you set off at dawn. It gets hot very fast and it would tire you out. Maria has already bought all you need for a couple of days, so you don't need to worry about that. We'll pick you up whenever we go to town, for as long as you stay. Alex's house isn't far from us and you can pop over whenever you like. I hope you'll soon get rid of that cough and then you can really enjoy Corsica.'

Hazel's eyes twinkled, and she studied the scene as the road wound gradually upward along.

'I wasn't certain if I was doing the right thing to come here, but now I'm glad. It's wonderful. So exotic, so different to anything I've ever seen before. There must be marvellous views from the town out to sea.'

He nodded.

'Yes, that's true, but the view from Alex's house is just as good.'

They left the town behind them and drove on for another 20 minutes or so until Anthony indicated towards a beaten pathway to their right.

'That leads to our house. I won't take you there now. I'm sure you'd like to see Alex's place first and relax a little. I'll pick you up again in a couple of hours. Maria wants you to come for a meal this evening.'

They drove down the pot-holed track, and were jostled and bumped until Mr Lorenzi stopped in front of a flight of steps cut into the rock.

'This is it. Alex has a local couple who keep the place ready and waiting, so don't be surprised if you suddenly see a man or a woman working around the house. Vincenzo and Teresa speak quite good English. They don't come every day, only as often as is needed. I'll fetch your luggage. Go on up. I'll join you in a minute.'

They got out and climbed the steps. Hazel stopped halfway, to get her breath back. It showed Catrin just how much Hazel needed this holiday away from home and all the work she did every day. She was still coughing badly.

Grey and dark brown brickwork lined the edges of steps in the rock. When Catrin reached the top, she found herself on a wide terrace running the length of the house. She looked to the side, into the distance, and saw wild countryside that ended abruptly, in mid-air. She guessed it was where the edge of the cliff began, and beyond that was nothing but the sea.

The house itself was magnificent. Built on two levels, she guessed before they went inside that the interior would be impressive.

Mr Lorenzi gave them a quick tour of the rooms on the lower level. The spacious living-room had white furniture and fittings, and a grey and white cube-shaped marble fireplace dominated one of the walls.

Catrin commented.

'A fireplace?'

He nodded.

'We get cool temperatures in winter here too, sometimes. An open fireplace is an added bonus.'

The floor-length windows along the length of the one wall faced the back of the house. There was a large kidney-shaped swimming pool on the nearest side of the wide stonework terrace. The turquoise water beckoned invitingly as soon as they saw it.

Mr Lorenzi chuckled when he noticed their amazed expressions.

'Nice, eh? Alex put the pool this side because it gets more shade in the afternoons. The other side, facing the sea, gets sunshine nearly all day long. There's a small private beach via some steps from the edge of the cliff. If you prefer sand to the pool, you might like to use that some days. It's not very big, but it's absolutely private. Be careful if you are not a good swimmer, there are tricky currents once you leave the enclosure of the rocks.'

Catrin couldn't help smiling as she looked around.

'It's fantastic. I love the design of the house and the way it blends with its surroundings. I think it has something to do with the shape or the colour.'

Hazel nodded.

'Like something out of a movie.'

He beamed.

'Yes, I think it's pretty fantastic, too. I'm proud of Alex and what he's achieved. The ideas and work he put into this place is unbelievable. Solar panels cover nearly all his energy needs although he has a generator that springs into action when necessary. The solar panels face out to sea further up the hill, and aren't a blot on the landscape.

'The water supply is a natural spring and he has reserve tanks underground. The spring water flows continually through the pool, making the use of chemicals unnecessary. Follow me. I'll show you the rest.'

The kitchen was full of gadgets, and a mixture of white surfaces and stainless steel. There was an adjoining utility room, and a pantry with lots of storage space and large freezers.

Climbing the open staircase, they found doors leading off a circular podium that overlooked the living-room. The doors led into various bedrooms and a couple of bathrooms. Furnishings were tasteful and in muted colours.

Catrin could tell at a glance that everything was expensive and carefully chosen. The rooms had a mixture of modern and antique furniture, and colourful paintings that she presumed were local scenes.

Catching her breath, she turned to Alex's father.

'Do we choose our room?'

'Yes, of course. Apart from the one right at the end over there.' He pointed to the door in question. 'That's Alex's private domain. Otherwise, it doesn't matter — take your pick. There are six altogether and two bathrooms. There's also a shower-room downstairs and a guest toilet. I'll show you how to use the air-conditioning and then I'll leave you to it.'

They followed him dutifully downstairs again and he explained how to use the controls on the air-conditioning.

'If you'll take my advice Hazel, don't set it too cool. If you are not used to it, there's a temptation to do so at first. If the difference between the outside temperatures and that of the inside is too much, it might cause you even more health problems. A couple of degrees difference is enough.'

Looking over his shoulder, and

listening carefully, Catrin nodded.

'Right. Well, I'll leave you to settle in. If there are any problems or questions, I'll solve them when I pick you up this evening. Alex told me to tell you to use anything you find. Will eight-thirty for nine be OK? Maria likes to eat late in the evening ever since we moved here. It's cooler at that time of day.'

They nodded and thanked him profusely and Hazel hugged him again. After he left, they went around the house again, exclaiming and full of approval.

'This is better than any five-star hotel,' Hazel commented. 'Wait until I get back and tell them about it at the Women's Institute meeting.'

Catrin laughed.

'Yes, it's incredible. We are in the wilds of Corsica, but this is pure luxury. You'll have to start taking photos, Hazel.' She looked at her more closely. 'I think it's a good idea for us to have a cup of tea on the terrace and then you can have a nap. You can unpack later. It was a long journey and a rest will do you good.'

Hazel didn't argue. Catrin could tell she was tired although she wouldn't admit it. They went back to the terrace bordering the swimming pool and Hazel settled under the oversize dark-blue sunshade. It took Catrin a couple of minutes to find what she needed in the kitchen.

Once the kettle boiled she carried the tray outside and sank down gratefully into one of the wickerwork chairs and their blue-and-white cushions. They drank their tea and both said they still couldn't believe their luck.

'I presumed that Alex was a good architect,' Catrin said, 'but not that he could produce something this good. The house is perfect, the surroundings are perfect, and he has combined them in such a way that they feel right. There's not another building in site, and the view is fantastic. On this side one looks towards the mountains, on the other side one looks out to sea.'

Hazel took a sip of tea.

'I always thought he was a special lad and would do something extraordinary. All this proves that he has.'

Hazel chose a bedroom next door to one of the bathrooms. Catrin chose the one on the other side, to keep the cleaning to a minimum.

Anthony had mentioned Vincenzo and his wife looked after the house, but Hazel declared firmly there was no need to take advantage of the situation and make more work than was necessary.

Once Hazel had gone for a rest, Catrin decided to explore and find her way down to the beach.

As she neared the cliff edge, the sea was an expanse of various shades of blue. The closer she came, the clearer she saw that today the sea was untroubled by the wind or unfriendly waves.

There was a cloudless sky and the scent of herbs floated around her as she picked her way carefully down the rough stone steps cut into the face of the rock.

The surface was uneven beneath her sandals and she held the side of the rough rock for safety. There was a small private cove at the bottom with coarse, light sand that felt hot, even under the protective soles of her sandals.

Catrin discarded her sandals and took a few steps across the sandy surface, to the shallow water at its edge.

She stood for a moment and was fascinated to notice after a while that some tiny silver fish were darting about her ankles. They shot off again when she moved her foot.

Back on the firm sand, she sat down and circled her knees with her arms, looking out to sea. There was a tiny ship moving slowly along the horizon. She wondered how far away it was.

It was a perfect place.

However much she might doubt Alex's motives about Aunt Hazel's land, there was no doubt in her mind that he was a talented architect who had built himself a faultless home in a perfect position.

The sun was hot on her shoulders and her commonsense told her not to linger. She got up and brushed away the sand from her cotton trousers.

Climbing back up the steps, she was almost envious of Hazel.

She'd be on her way back to the muted tones and cooler weather of England again the day after tomorrow.

Meeting Maria

By the time Hazel emerged, the sun had almost disappeared in a blaze of glory. Catrin had unpacked her small bag and was sitting on the terrace reading a book in the shade.

Hazel smiled at her.

'Isn't this wonderful? I already feel better.'

'You look better, too. It was a long journey, you are not in top condition and you flew for the first time in your life. I'm sure this stay will do you the world of good, though. Do you think you can manage the return journey on your own? Otherwise I'll come and fetch you.'

Hazel straightened.

'Don't worry. I watched carefully how you got us here. If Anthony drives me to the airport and helps me with my suitcase to the right checking in desk, then I only need to go through passport and customs controls. As long as I get on the right plane, I'll be fine.'

Catrin laughed softly.

'There's no chance of you getting on the wrong plane — they check your ticket and boarding card. I'll meet you in London. When you get off the plane just follow the others.'

Hazel looked at the pool.

'I haven't swum for donkey's years, but it's something you don't forget. I packed my swimsuit and I'm going for a dip. What about you?'

Catrin stood up.

'Good idea! I put a bikini in my bag in case we were near a beach. I didn't think that we'd have a private pool! You'll have to use plenty of sun block every day, Hazel. I noticed this afternoon how much stronger the sun is here. You'll get sunburned in no time at all if you don't.'

'I've brought plenty of high factor sun-cream, so I should be all right.'

An hour later, when daylight was

beginning to fade, they felt refreshed after capering around in the turquoise water, and both of them declared they were hungry.

'There's no point in us eating anything now. Anthony will be picking us up in an hour, and Maria will be upset if we turn up without an appetite. By the time we're dressed and ready to go he'll be here.'

Catrin didn't have a great choice in what she could wear, but she packed a shift dress with narrow shoulder straps that withstood the trials of constricted packing very well. It was pale lemon and simple in style and it suited her.

She applied some mascara and lipstick, brushed her hair and grabbed her shoulder bag before she hurried downstairs to wait with Hazel for Anthony to take them to his home.

He was on time and they climbed into the same vehicle as before. He shook his head when they asked about locking the house.

'No-one lives near here, and even if they did people are very honest. Alex only locks it if he knows he'll be away for a long time.'

He looked across at Hazel.

'You look a bit better already. Maria is looking forward to seeing you so much. You know how often we've asked you to come on a visit. Why did you wait until you were ill?'

Hazel laughed.

'I'm here now, Anthony, and I'm looking forward to seeing Maria again after all this time. We were good pals when you were living in the village.'

'You were more than a good pal to us. We'll never forget that.'

Anthony was driving at a high speed, and Catrin wondered how he managed to find the way in the darkness. There were no markings or helpful indications.

'We never forgot the way you helped when Maria fell down the stairs and had to stay in bed for weeks. You came every day, did the housework, did the shopping, kept Maria happy, and you even kept coming to help her afterwards, even though she could get up and hobble about.'

'It made us good friends. I always liked Maria. She is down to earth and honest, and she has a wicked sense of humour. Remember how she knitted purple earmuffs for Billy Rainer's cows?'

He chuckled as the headlights cut through the darkness and they bowled along.

'Yes, he had quite a shock when he went into the shed and saw them all lined up with their earmuffs on. I can't even remember why she did it. Maria is like that.'

'I think she had a discussion with him about whether cows get earache when they stand around in cold winds!'

He laughed.

'He thought it was a great joke. In fact, I think it made him a celebrity in the local pub for ages after.'

Catrin had never heard the story

before. When they reached the old farmhouse, she was very curious to find out what Alex's mother was like.

Maria had a round, jovial face and she embraced Hazel as soon as she left the car. She squeezed her tight and kissed her cheek.

'Hazel, it is wonderful to see you again. I'm so glad Alex could persuade you to spend some time here.'

Hazel relaxed because she was with friends.

'This is my niece, Catrin. She volunteered to bring me here. I flew for the first time and I was glad of her company and her help.'

Catrin held out her hand.

'Hello, Mrs Lorenzi. I'm pleased to meet you.'

Maria studied the younger woman carefully, and smiled.

'Maria, please. Come inside. We'll eat on the terrace at the back of the house. I hope you are hungry.'

She bustled ahead of them, and they were soon sitting at a table beneath a covering framework of wild olives with a dish of appetisers and a bowl of fat juicy olives. Catrin could see the stars between the gaps. The night air was mild and gentle on her skin.

Anthony opened a bottle of wine and Catrin noticed how Maria was still considering her carefully. They settled down to chat. Anthony filled their glasses.

'This is a wine from Corsica. Not an exclusive one, but excellent in its own way.'

They lifted their glasses and toasted each other. Maria turned to Catrin.

'Hazel mentioned you often, but we never met, did we?'

'No, I don't think so. My visits were usually short ones. Unless we needed something badly I never went to the village very often, so we weren't very likely to meet, were we? Now that Hazel has explained where you used to live, I do remember your garden, though. It was always a riot of colour.'

Maria looked satisfied.

'I can't achieve half as much here, it's too hot. My English garden is one of the things I miss.' She picked up her glass again. 'Hazel was always happy whenever you came to visit.'

Hazel nodded.

'And she still comes regularly, bless her. Catrin is a great help and support.'

Maria nodded. She asked about Catrin's job, where she lived, if she was engaged, married, what her friends did, where her family was, and if she enjoyed travelling.

Hazel knew her old friend very well. She beamed at Catrin and her eyes sparkled. Catrin gathered this was Maria's normal way of assessing new acquaintances.

Catrin could understand why Hazel liked her. She was forthright and had a very friendly attitude.

Curiosity satisfied, Maria pushed back her chair and declared it was time to eat.

When she moved into the house, Hazel automatically followed to help.

Watching her, Catrin thought her stride was already jauntier, and realised how good the holiday would be for her.

They had a delicious meal, and even Hazel ate everything without asking too many questions about what it was. Anthony supplied some comments anyway.

'Maria's fish soup is made from the local fish, and the pork fillets and stuffed vegetables are another of her specialities.'

'It is all extremely delicious,' Catrin said. 'I read in a travel magazine on the plane that Corsican food is a mixture of Italian and French dishes, because Corsica once belonged to both of those countries and it influenced developments.'

Anthony nodded.

'Centuries ago the local population lived mainly on products from chestnuts because there was no other choice. Thankfully those days are long gone.'

The evening passed pleasantly, with exchanges of past memories, promises to visit each other regularly, to take her shopping, and show Hazel the island's tourist attractions whenever she felt strong enough to cope with a day out in the sun.

'Keep out of the sun until you are used to the heat,' Maria warned her. 'There should be enough food at Alex's house until Monday. We'll go shopping together on Monday — early, when it's cooler.'

'I was just thinking that your house is quite a long way from Alex's place,' Hazel commented.

Anthony laughed and cut himself a generous portion of the local cheese.

'It is by road, but not if you walk up the hill behind the house, and down the other side. Maria's father owned all the land around here. This is his original farmhouse. I've just modernised it.

'Alex asked for the land on the other side, facing the sea, and we were delighted when he built his house there. Several clients have commissioned him after they looked around his house. I only had a small business. Alex has achieved so much more already.'

Catrin relaxed as insects buzzed around the lanterns. Hazel was going to have a good time.

Unexpected Encounter

Next morning, Catrin woke to the perfume of Corsica flowing through the open window. The white gauze-like material moved like the waves of the ocean, back and forth.

She stretched lazily and enjoyed the knowledge she had a whole day ahead of her to relish her surroundings. It was early; just six o'clock but there wasn't a moment to spare.

In her bikini, she grabbed a towel and ran downstairs. The house was silent and Hazel was still in her room, presumably fast asleep.

Catrin slid into the blue waters of the pool. It was cool at first but after a few minutes, it felt extremely refreshing. The water flowed over her skin like silk.

The sun was still shining softly on this side of the house although shadows were already gathering along the walls. She swam a few lengths and turned on to her back to float for a while. That was how she felt, floating in mid-air with reality far away.

Turning to swim again, out of the corner of her eye, she noticed someone on the terrace. Expecting to see Hazel, she was shocked when she saw Alex sitting in one of the chairs. He was watching her and Catrin spluttered as her open mouth took in water.

'Alex! What . . . what are you doing here?'

His smile was startlingly white in his tanned face.

'What do you think? This does happen to be my house.'

She swam back to a position where she could stand.

'Yes, of course,' she responded. 'I realise that. I mean, no-one expected you. Your parents invited us for a meal last night, and they didn't say you were coming.' She pushed her wet hair back off her face and waited.

'Because they didn't know. I generally come and go as time allows. I decided to fly in on the spur of the moment to see that Hazel was OK.'

'I thought you were too busy. How did you get here? It's quite a distance from the airport. I didn't hear a taxi — or any vehicle for that matter.'

He laughed.

'Questions, questions! I was on the last flight of the day. I have a dilapidated Renault in a garage near the airport. I parked it a little way from the house when I got here, because I didn't want to disturb or frighten both of you in the night.'

Catrin coloured.

'I'm sorry. I must sound rude. It is just an unexpected surprise to see you, that's all.'

'Not an unpleasant surprise, I hope?'

Catrin felt too confused to declare otherwise, and she hurried to reply.

'No, of course not.'

He looked around.

'I gather Hazel isn't up yet?'

'No, I don't think so.'

'I usually have breakfast out on the terrace. Will you join me? Somehow I don't think it will be long before Hazel joins us.'

He got up and came to the edge of the pool. He held out his hand.

Catrin accepted defeat and knew refusing would be silly and discourteous. He pulled her out with ease.

She felt exposed as he studied her top to toe. She wasn't ashamed of her slim figure even though she wished it was curvier in some places, but she didn't enjoy his surveillance. It was embarrassing.

She grabbed the towel from the nearby chair and wrapped it round herself like a sarong.

His eyes twinkled knowingly.

'I suggest you get dressed. You'll be more comfortable in something that's dry. I'll start the coffee.'

Catrin dashed upstairs and showered quickly before changing again into her cotton trousers and a fresh top. She felt irritated, and at a disadvantage. She hadn't even been polite enough to praise his house. She'd been too busy coping with her surprise at seeing him.

For a moment, she thought about knocking on Hazel's door and waiting for her, but that would just be to avoid being alone with him, and why should she do that?

A few seconds later, she straightened her shoulders and skipped down the stairs. Her hair was still wet but she'd brushed it into shape.

He'd set the table with tempting items: fresh orange juice, succulent melon, local cheeses, dried sausage, and yoghurt. He was munching on some bread. He gestured to the opposite chair.

'There are other things in the pantry. Cereals, honey, frozen bread rolls . . . '

'No, this is fine.' She sat down and looked across the table. 'I haven't told you that I think your house is fabulous.'

She was slightly out of breath because of him sitting opposite but she wanted to be honest.

'I can't remember seeing a private home I liked more. The position is perfect. It's so private with the sea in one direction, and the mountain in the other.'

His eyes brightened with pleasure.

'I'm glad you like it. I acted very egoistically when I built it and the bank manager nearly had a heart attack a couple of times.'

'It's perfect, inside and out. Thank you for letting Hazel stay here. I'm sure it will help a lot. She looks better already.'

He nodded.

'I presume that you're flying out again tomorrow?'

'Yes, back to the grindstone. We're in the middle of preparations for a new exhibition in the autumn. There are lots of meetings, negotiations, discussions, and arguments still to get through before things actually start moving.'

'You like your work?'

His face had a clean, chiselled look

that impressed her. Even in a navy polo shirt and white shorts, she was conscious of his tall athletic physique.

He leaned back and cradled his hands around his glass of cold orange juice.

'Yes, I love it. It's very rewarding. We have historical exhibitions, events to bring kids closer to history, exhibitions of ancient and modern paintings, and we support local archaeological digs, historical displays or such events in any way we can.'

Catrin was too curious not to ask.

'I was wondering if you think of the UK as your home or Corsica.'

He laughed softly.

'My official headquarters are in London, and the majority of my commissions, so far, come from France. I love Corsica, and when I have any spare time, I spend it here . . . '

Hazel's arrival interrupted them. She stopped in the doorway when she saw him.

'Alex! Good heavens! What are you

doing here? When did you arrive?'

He pulled out a neighbouring chair.

'I got in last night. Too late to disturb you. It's only a flying visit. I have a meeting in Paris on Monday morning, but I wanted to check you arrived safely and had everything you need. I know my parents will keep an eye on you, but I thought you might want something and wouldn't mention it to them.'

Hazel sat down.

'No, I have everything. Who could grumble about anything when they're staying in this place? It is wonderful.'

'Good.'

'I'm going shopping with your mother on Monday even though your fridge is already full with more than I need.' Hazel looked at Catrin. 'You're early this morning.'

'Yes, I think it has something to do with the air. You know that I'm not an early bird usually.'

As Hazel settled and started to have her breakfast, Catrin was finishing her coffee.

'I'm going to explore a little, before it gets too hot,' she said. 'I only have today to look around. Want to come?'

Hazel brushed her words aside.

'I have plenty of time. Explore on your own.'

'You can't get lost if you stick to the paths,' Alex told her. 'Use something like the tip of the hill behind the house as a landmark.'

'Why don't you go with her, Alex?' Hazel suggested. 'I'm sure Catrin would enjoy strolling around with someone who knows the locality. When you get back I'll make us something light for lunch.'

Alex looked at her questioningly.

Catrin could only think that when he came here he wanted to relax, not act as a tourist guide. She was about to decline when he spoke first.

'My pleasure, if Catrin would like it.'

Confused by her feelings, she nodded quickly.

'Yes, of course. If you have the time, and don't mind.'

The path was dusty, clearly demonstrating this was a landscape where there was a scarcity of regular rain showers. Thick herblike vegetation made up the undergrowth. There was a strong aroma in the air, typical for the island.

She stayed at his side although the so-called path was barely wide enough. She enjoyed her surroundings and the mere fact that she was here walking with him.

He gestured with a sweep of his hand.

'Do you like it, or is it too wild, too untamed? Some parts of the island are much greener — it depends upon where you are. The mountains are skirted by pine forests, green oaks, and chestnut trees in the lower regions.'

'I like it. It's so different to the English countryside. There's a fragrance in the air everywhere. What is it? I don't see many flowering plants.'

He smiled.

'You can smell the Fleur de Corse, an

aromatic plant, a living potpourri that grows all over Corsica. Twenty percent of the ground is scrubland, the maquis. Depending on whether the maquis is a lower, middle, or upper one, the plants even have a varying smell and their own individual oil. The perfume industry uses the plants, and people have used them for centuries for medicinal and other purposes. Bonaparte said he knew he was home when he could smell the Fleur de Corse.'

'Are we close to the cliffs here?'

'Yes, they're just over there.'

He looked across and she found she couldn't hold his gaze. She glanced down quickly and let the moment pass.

'Shall we sit down by those big rocks over there? We'll be in the shade. You'll get sunburn if we aren't careful. We'll have to remind Hazel, too.'

She nodded, although she would have been just as happy to carry on. They found a shady spot and he turned to face her.

She took off her hat and stroked away

the moisture on her forehead.

'Did you spend much time on Corsica when you were growing up, or start coming back when your parents settled here?'

'I spent most of the school holidays with my grandparents at the farm when I was growing up. Even when I started helping my father in the business, I tried to come back as often as I could. My grandparents were an important part of my growing up. Coming here regularly helped me to become fluent in French and it sharpened my Italian. That has helped me in my professional life.

'I wish they were still around and I could pay back some of the care and interest they showered on me. They had a frugal life and worked hard physically trying to keep body and soul together.'

She looked around.

'The landscape is pretty harsh, isn't it? Farming anything here, then or now, must be difficult.'

'My grandparents had lots of olive

and fig trees, they grew vegetables, and they kept goats for milk and cheese. They traded the cheese and vegetables at the local market and made olive oil. These days, farmers concentrate on wine and pigs.

'There's plenty of tourism, too, and it seems to grow whenever I come. I seldom go out when I'm here. I don't need to race around and I know this part of the island like the back of my hand. I know the people and they know me.'

Catrin leaned forward. She could see the Mediterranean Sea on the horizon, but she couldn't see the edge of the cliffs. A gust of wind grabbed her hat and he reached out for it. He fitted it back on her head and his fingers brushed against her temple.

Their eyes met and Catrin was unprepared for the thrill she felt.

She told herself it meant nothing. She reminded herself about Aunt Hazel's fields. She looked quickly away.

'Thank you. Do you come to this

spot often?' she asked, trying to sound casual.

He shrugged.

'Not any more. I used to. Generally to meet up with some friends from the village. It's a shady spot and there are often cool winds. One of us always managed to bring wine and some cheese.'

He looked behind her head, and Catrin could see how his expression changed.

'Sophia!' He stood up quickly.

A young woman with ebony hair, olive skin, and curvy figure was coming towards them with a basket on her arm. She quickened her pace when she saw Alex and her smile was warm and generous. She gave Catrin a passing glance but she concentrated on him. He embraced her tightly, kissing her cheek.

They exchanged a couple of sentences in French. Catrin's French was rusty. She just about managed to understand that the one questioned the other about what they were doing there.

Remembering Catrin, he turned to her with his arm still around Sophia's shoulder.

'This is Sophia, an old friend from way back when.'

Catrin nodded and smiled.

'Hello.'

'Catrin is the niece of a friend of mine,' Alex added. 'Hazel — you've heard me talking about Hazel, haven't you? Catrin brought Hazel here for a visit.'

Sophia said hello and smiled but the smile didn't quite reach her eyes.

'Are you staying with Hazel?'

Catrin could tell she hoped she wasn't.

'No, I'm not staying long. I'm off home again tomorrow.'

Reassured, Sophia turned her attention to Alex again.

'But you're staying longer, I hope. We haven't seen you in the village for ages. Paulo mentioned you the other day, and wondered where you were and what you were doing.'

Alex laughed softly.

'I'm island-hopping at the moment. From Britain to France, from France to Corsica, from Corsica to France and on to Sicily. When I have more time I'll call, promise. How is your business going?' He turned to Catrin. 'Sophia has a boutique in a tourist centre near here.'

Sophia looked smug.

'It's doing well. People seem to like what I have on offer and I've started to include products made on the island. I've found a brilliant bag-maker who makes extremely stylish items. I can sell her bags faster than she can produce them.'

'I'm not surprised. You always had an eye for fashion and what will sell.'

He held her at arm's length and considered her red Capri pants and loose white sleeveless blouse. For a moment Catrin resented how friendly and relaxed they were with each other.

She got up quickly and brushed her trousers. She felt hot and untidy and

Sophia's well-groomed appearance didn't help to banish that thought.

'Where are you going?' Alex asked Sophia.

'My mother wants some of Franco's cheese. I offered to fetch it before I go to the shop.' She considered him and tilted her head to the side. 'A couple of us are meeting up at the beach this evening. Why don't you come?' She saw how his brows lifted and how he looked at Catrin. 'Catrin too, of course,' she added hastily. 'It will be like old times again.'

'Um, perhaps.'

Sophia reached up and ran her finger along his chin.

'Make an effort, Alex. Just for me!' she added coyly.

Silently, Catrin turned away and walked towards the cliff edge. She was glad to feel the fresh sea breezes on her skin.

Thoughts Running Wild

Catrin noticed how Sophia raised her hand in farewell. She wasn't sure who the intended recipient was, so she nodded in her direction. There was no reason for her to be impolite.

'Would you like to go this evening? It's only a casual get-together.' Alex asked her.

Before he could continue, she cut in.

'They're your friends. Please don't bother about me. Do as you please. I can spend a comfortable evening with Hazel.'

His expression was neutral.

'I'd like you to come and I'm sure Hazel won't mind.' She was still hesitant and he noticed. 'If you don't want to, then I won't bother, either.'

Then she would be responsible for keeping him from his seeing his friends. She cleared her throat.

'Only if you are absolutely sure I won't get in the way.'

'I'm sure.' He looked up at the sun in its zenith. 'Let's go back; a swim will cool you down.'

She smiled.

'I came to help Hazel settle in, and here I am gallivanting around the countryside with you, and swimming in the azure waters of your private swimming pool.'

He appraised her with close interest.

'Why not just enjoy whatever the day brings?'

He reached up and gently touched her shoulder. Her skin tingled at his touch and Catrin told herself not to be silly. She had difficulty not to jerk away. She didn't want to show him the effect it had on her.

She couldn't afford to be friends or show any special interest in him, not even a casual friendship, until she knew exactly if and why he'd offered to buy Hazel's land.

She remained silent most of the time

as they made their way back to the house. She didn't feel awkward in his company, but she was wary about exactly how much he interested her.

She hardly knew the man but for some reason her thoughts about him were running wild.

As they reached the bottom of the steps leading up to the terrace there was a man with a rake coming down towards them. Alex lifted his hand and said something to him in what sounded a strange language, but she presumed was Corsican.

He gestured towards Catrin and the man doffed his hat briefly. Catrin smiled at him. He was deeply tanned, dressed in tattered dungarees, and wore tough-looking working boots.

'This is Vincenzo,' Alex explained. 'He and his wife keep their eye on the house for me. I'll have to remind Hazel not to do any housework, otherwise Teresa will be offended. Vincenzo keeps the undergrowth around the house under control, cleans the pool, and does that sort of thing.'

Vincenzo nodded and lifted the rake on to his shoulder before he walked away.

'What luxury! I expect Hazel will get itchy fingers. She's not used to doing nothing, so you had better warn her. If she reads, gets visits from your parents and goes with them on trips now and then, she'll be able to fill her time in very well.'

Catrin welcomed the cool when they were indoors and went towards the stairs.

'I'm just going to have a cool shower. See you later.'

Feeling fresh again afterwards, she skipped downstairs and looked for Hazel. She was outside under the shade of an umbrella talking to Alex on the main terrace. There was fresh orange juice and glasses on the table.

When she joined them, he gestured to the juice.

'Help yourself!'

'Alex just told me about meeting his

friend and the invitation to join them this evening,' Hazel said. 'Go. I'll have an early night with a book.' She looked at Catrin wistfully. 'I wish you could stay longer. What time do you have to leave tomorrow?'

'I have to be at the airport early tomorrow afternoon. When the plane gets into London I'll have plenty of time to drive home before it gets dark.'

Alex smiled broadly.

'Air France?' She nodded. 'I'm on that flight, too. I have to be in a meeting in Paris for first thing on Monday morning.'

'Really?' she murmured, feeling flustered. 'What a coincidence.'

Alex rubbed his hands together.

'That makes things easier for Dad. He won't need to drive to the airport.' He got up. 'Right, that's settled. I'll just let my father know about tomorrow.'

Hazel thanked him again for his hospitality and kindness. He brushed her words aside.

'If it puts you back on the road to

feeling better, that's fine by me.'

Catrin watched him as he disappeared into the house. His every movement and his appearance reminded her that he was a very attractive man. Her brain reminded her that she was still suspicious of him, and his lean and craggy looks attracted other women, too. There was no point in losing any sleep over him. He moved in a different world.

Her only concern at present was Hazel. They chatted easily for a while until Hazel left her for an afternoon nap.

When Alex reappeared, he threw himself into the chair opposite. Catrin told herself her heart was only beating faster because of his sudden appearance. She caught the scent of his aftershave.

Without any warning, she realised suddenly that she liked him very much. She didn't want to analyse how much. He could be trying to cheat Hazel out of her land.

* * *

Wearing her yellow dress again, Catrin found the journey to the beach was short. Alex drove across barely visible tracks and she sat bouncing along beside him until they joined a road with a proper surface. It was probably a short walk in the daytime but it was rough and more difficult in the semi-darkness.

He adjusted his step to stay at Catrin's side as they wandered towards the small beach with its white sand. There was a distinctive sound of music and voices when they passed through the simple bistro facing the sea and came out on to a small terrace. Some older people sat at wooden tables gossiping. A couple of them greeted Alex and he returned their greetings without actually stopping.

He propelled Catrin onwards, with his hand in the small of her back until they could see a crowd of younger people gathered together further along the beach. There was a general sense of pleasure as glasses clinked, and laughter wafted towards them on the evening air like a comforting breeze.

As they reached the group, Alex seemed relaxed. His arm lay casually around her shoulder when they came to a standstill.

A woman with a modern short hairstyle came towards them with a tray of empty glasses. She looked at the girl at Alex's side with dark, interested eyes.

'Hello! Lovely to see you again, Alex, we don't see you often any more. How are you?'

'Fine. And you?'

She nodded.

'Me, too!' She put the tray down on a nearby table.

He obliged the unknown woman with an introduction and she glanced directly at Catrin.

'I'll take care of Catrin! She'll get bored listening to everyone catching up on news.' He checked Catrin's reaction, she nodded, and he strolled off towards the others.

'I'm Carlotta.'

She patted Catrin's arm reassuringly and Catrin relaxed.

'I'll introduce you to some of the others,' Carlotta offered. 'I don't think you know anyone, do you?'

She tucked her hand under Catrin's elbow and guided her across a stretch of warm sand to a firmer area of the beach bordering the ocean.

As they progressed, Carlotta chatted pleasantly with Catrin about the village.

'How do you like Corsica? Are you enjoying your visit?'

Catrin nodded enthusiastically and smiled.

'Very much! Who wouldn't! I'm only here for two days but I love what I've seen of it.'

Carlotta looked pleased.

'It does have negative sides, like the storms and high unemployment, or the Mistral, but on the whole, I agree. I've always loved living here.'

'Were you born here?'

She laughed gently.

'No. I come from Milan. I met Ronaldo on vacation; he talked me into coming for a visit. The result was that I instantly uprooted and replanted myself here. I loved it here from day one.'

They approached others near rocks where bottles and glasses stood haphazardly for people to help themselves.

Catrin noticed Alex's tall figure was coming towards them. Her pulse jumped around erratically and she calmed herself as he drew closer. They exchanged smiles.

Carlotta looked at them closely.

'I'll leave Catrin in your care. I think I need to get some more white wine.' She'd noted the fleeting change in Alex's expression as his eyes focused on Catrin.

Carlotta had often wondered why someone as attractive and successful as Alex wasn't married. She presumed he was too busy with his job, but some instinct told her this girl might change all that.

There was something special in his expression.

She turned towards the café and thought about Sophia. Sophia had always been in love with Alex and whenever the gang met up and Alex was there, she continued to give him plenty of encouragement. She'd try again this evening if she got the chance.

Carlotta just wondered if Sophia loved Alex for what he was, or if she saw him as her ticket to a comfortable lifestyle.

It Ended in a Kiss

Catrin studied Alex's face in the lengthening darkness and forced herself to remain calm.

'Nice meeting your friends again?' It was a trivial remark, but all that came to mind.

His dark brown eyes seemed almost black as they regarded her, and she saw a secretive smile soften his lips.

'Yes, it's OK! Good, in fact.' He held out his hand, palm up, and she hesitatingly placed hers in his. 'Come and meet some more of them!'

She was very conscious of him holding her hand as he led her toward another group of people. He introduced her as they strolled around and Catrin was pleased to find most of them could speak English very well.

'This is Toni.'

A good-looking man with a warm

smile acknowledged Catrin.

'You don't have a drink,' he pointed out. He took her free hand and led the way.

Forced to release her, Alex heard someone shout his name and he moved towards the caller.

Toni told Catrin to choose something so she picked up a tall glass, filled it with a little Campari and topped it up with orange juice. The glass felt cold in her hand.

'What do you do, Toni?'

'Do? I'm a pilot. Only transport planes at present, but I hope to fly for a commercial airline one day. Do you know anyone else here?'

Catrin shook her head.

'No-one apart from Alex and Sophia. We met her this morning, when we were out for a walk.'

He grinned.

'It never takes Sophia long to appear on the scene when she knows Alex is home. What do you think of him? Are you his girlfriend?'

'No, I'm not. I like him. We get on OK but I don't know him very well.'

'Oh, really? That's good. He is so darned successful that it puts the rest of us to shame. Most people, especially the women, think he's wonderful.' Toni grinned.

Catrin tossed her hair and laughed softly.

'Even wonderful people have weak points.'

She took a sip of her drink and felt almost carefree. When she was with Alex, there was more tension in the air. Toni was clearly used to flirting with women and he was hoping to put Alex in the shade.

He laughed.

'Tell me more!'

'Oh, I just don't know him well enough — and I don't like gossiping about people I hardly know. I'm only here because he offered his house to my aunt for a visit. It was her first flight ever, so I brought her. Alex turned up unexpectedly this morning. I'm going home tomorrow. I only met Alex once before.'

'I heard about your aunt coming, from Alex's father. I met him in town a day or two ago.' He smiled when he saw her head tilt to the side, a questioning expression on her face. 'You can't keep anything secret in this place. Your aunt is ill, isn't she?'

She nodded and loved the way warm breezes were caressing her face.

'Chest trouble, but this sunshine will do her a world of good!'

He nodded.

'It's a pity that you're leaving tomorrow. We could have gone out for a meal or done something else. At least it sounds like you haven't fallen under Alex's spell yet. I must admit, he's never ruthless when it comes to women, but most of the single women I know would fall in line with anything he wanted, good or bad — just to catch him.'

A movement behind Catrin's head caught Toni's attention. Catrin wasn't very surprised to turn her head and find Alex was standing behind her. He must have heard the tail end of their conversation.

Catrin's colour heightened. He moved around to face her, skimming her features with dark, expressive eyes.

'Thank you for your glowing descriptions, Toni. I'm pinching her again now.' He caught Catrin's wrist, and pulled her gently but firmly away. Her drink splashed dangerously in her free hand.

Catrin looked back at Toni with wide eyes. She didn't understand Alex's irritation, but. she had no choice but to follow.

Alex slowed his pace when they reached the edge of the group. They stood facing the sea and could hear the sound of the waves crashing on to the beach. It gave Catrin time to catch her breath and concentrate properly.

He regarded her for a moment; and they stared silently at each other in the half shadows. Catrin looked over his head and saw the moon rising like a silver coin in the sky. He gave her a tight smile that finished abruptly.

She blinked, and felt wary. His voice was deceivingly soft, and his eyes glinted dangerously. Alex straightened.

'Don't take any notice of Toni. He tries to impress any girl that crosses his path with his joking and his job as a pilot. He's a flirt.'

'Is he?' Catrin wondered why Alex decided to warn her. 'I didn't take him seriously. He was just chatting and trying to entertain me.'

He moved a few steps away and picked up a can of cold beer from a rock pool. It was cold in his hand and he dented it as he pulled the tab. It made a hissing sound and some of the liquid poured down the side, wetting his fingers. He lifted it to his lips, took a long mouthful, then wiped his lips with the back of his hand.

'You seemed enthralled and I thought I should forewarn you.'

'Alex, I'm going home tomorrow. I'll

never see Toni again. He's not likely to kidnap me. I don't know why you imagine anything he says will impress me.'

She saw his shoulders shrug in the semi-darkness and then he straightened.

'Then perhaps I judged wrong and barged in? Sorry!' He gave her a swift glance, and then sauntered off.

She wondered what was wrong. Was it bad for her to talk to a strange man on her own? Perhaps Corsican conventions were austere. Or perhaps Toni had a girlfriend and Alex wanted to intervene before Toni went too far?

Catrin took a deep breath and stared up at the numerous stars now winking in the sky. She hung on to her glass more tightly, and swallowed the lump in her throat. Perhaps Alex just saw it as some kind of personal provocation. Who knows why he reacted like that.

Catrin only hoped she could completely ignore her own growing attraction for him. Even during the moments when they differed about something, she felt a magnetism she'd never experienced before.

She was tempted to look for a quiet spot where she could fade into the shadows and wait patiently until it was time to go home, but she forced herself to join the others gathering round a bonfire of driftwood.

She cradled her glass, and listened politely to strangers who talked about people and things that meant nothing to her. The way the group was acting also showed her that there weren't exacting rules about behaviour. Many were fooling around.

Alex was standing with Sophia at his side. The salted wood sent bright blue sparks soaring into the sky. Whenever Catrin eyed the two of them across the gathering, Sophia was hanging on his every word as well as his arm. He did nothing to discourage her.

Catrin concentrated on the brown-eyed, six-foot giant of a man who was talking to her about his vineyard. He asked her about her job, about herself. Catrin was grateful to him.

Who needed Alex Lorenzi?

★ ★ ★

Alex resisted the temptation to study her in the flickering light of the fire. It was more difficult than he imagined. He liked intelligent women who weren't coy and didn't cling. Catrin fitted that description. He felt annoyed when he heard her laughing with Geraldo.

He shifted his weight and disentangled Sophia's arm. Admittedly, he hadn't acted considerately. He'd been boorish and rude. He'd never liked Toni much, and he was irritated when he found them together and heard Toni discuss him with Catrin.

He didn't understand why she affected him as she did. He wasn't generally someone who acted childishly. He reluctantly admitted he'd felt a twinge of envy when he saw her with Toni.

★　　★　　★

Catrin slipped away from the crowd gathered around the fire and went back towards the wooden bistro to sit down on a nearby wall. She relaxed and enjoyed the sound of the ocean and the atmosphere. She was startled when she looked up and found him standing in front of her, his hands stuck in his pockets.

'Ready?'

'You don't have to call it a day because of me,' she said, flustered. 'I'm perfectly happy and enjoying myself. The sound of the sea is very relaxing, and it's like being on holiday. If I knew how to get back to the house without getting lost, I'd walk.'

He gave her a crooked smile and held out his hand.

'I'm sorry I butted in just now. You're old enough to make up your own mind about Toni or anyone else.'

She had no choice but to take his hand as he pulled her to her feet. She brushed the skirt of her dress and felt herself blush.

'There's no need to apologise. It wasn't important.'

He looked back towards the others.

'I'm ready if you are.'

Catrin was glad things were back to normal. They drove off without fare-wells. After a while, he left the road and drove into the darkness and the scrubland.

'I've only had one beer,' he commented. 'The surface is causing all the jiggling about.'

She laughed.

'I know that from the trip with your father.'

'Oh, yes, I forgot.'

'I'm glad you're driving. I'm sure I'd end up lost among the bushland or I'd drive off the cliff.'

'Heaven forbid! If you lived here, you'd soon get used to it I'm sure.'

There was a companionable silence until they reached home. He helped her out of the car and as he gave her his hand, she felt what she could only describe as a thrill. They walked towards the steps. He turned towards her suddenly and took her face between his hands.

She couldn't see his face properly, but when he lowered his head and kissed her, her limbs seemed to turn to liquid. It was a brief sensation but it created the most extraordinary effect on her. She'd never experienced anything similar before.

She didn't resist and looked into his shadowed face. His eyes were brilliant in the dark. Then without any explanation, he stepped away.

'Goodnight, Catrin!' he said softly. 'Sleep well.'

High Flying Journey

Next morning, time flew. Catrin was never alone with Alex and couldn't make up her mind if that was good or bad.

'Why did you kiss me? What did it mean?' These weren't questions you slipped into a normal conversation and Catrin would have been too embarrassed to try.

She went for a swim in the pool, followed by a leisurely breakfast with Hazel. Alex joined them and smiled at them both. Catrin decided that he had a brilliant smile. It was sudden and genuine.

Alex and Catrin exchanged glances across the table. They didn't avoid each other, but were swift to attend to Hazel, and only talk about generalities. Hazel asked if they'd enjoyed the evening and they both said yes, without offering many details.

It felt bizarre to face Alex across the table and not know what he thought about her. She knew it was impossible to ask him now without generating awkwardness.

After an early lunch and a shared coffee break later, she packed her bag again. When Alex suggested they left early, she was ready to go. With a flurried farewell and hugs, Catrin promised Hazel she would phone when she was home and that she would call every other day to see how she was.

Hazel beamed at them.

'Don't worry. Anthony and Maria are picking me up tomorrow morning to take me shopping. I'm used to being on my own and this place is wonderful for just relaxing.'

She stood at the top of the steps to see them off. Catrin looked back and waved until they were out of sight.

'She'll be all right,' he said, looking ahead and holding the steering wheel firmly on the bumpy road. 'I'm sure my mum and dad will keep a close eye on her.'

Catrin settled and nodded. She felt the magnetism of his attraction when he was so close, especially when she remembered his kisses last night. He seemed to have forgotten it. She tried not to lean in his direction as the car bumped and swerved its way back to the main road.

A dizzy current raced through her if she looked at his profile so she tried to keep her gaze straight ahead. They exchanged small talk, or he pointed out something of interest on the way. He didn't refer to last night at all, and Catrin followed his lead. She concluded it meant nothing to him.

He drove straight to the airport and drew up outside departures. Getting out, he deposited their bags on a nearby trolley.

'Could you hang on to mine until I get back? There's still plenty of time before we need to check in. I'll be back as soon as I've garaged the car.'

Catrin stood next to the bags.

'Of course. See you inside.'

She pushed the trolley through the sliding doors without looking back. She sat down opposite the Air France check-in counter and ten minutes later, she saw him coming towards her. He smiled and her intention to remain blase vanished. She smiled back.

After they'd completed the formalities, she realised he had a first-class ticket, and she was in economy. Once the boarding call came he joined the handful of first-class passengers. She was a little surprised that he didn't say goodbye although he did look back and lift his boarding card before he finally disappeared from sight.

Joining the other economy passengers going on board, she still hadn't made up her mind if she cared enough about him to wish she could get to know him properly.

Finding her seat, she made herself comfortable and waited while everyone else settled. The plane was only half full and the seats next to her were empty. Alex was suddenly standing alongside.

He held out his hand.

'Come with me.'

More than surprised, she kept her voice low.

'I'm economy. The crew . . . '

There was a glimmer of humour in his eyes.

'I've already cleared it. I often travel this route. I know the air hostess, and I explained you are a good friend. Do you have anything in the luggage rack?'

Bowled along by events, Catrin shook her head, and as he pulled her to her feet, she quickly grabbed her shoulder bag before he led the way through the curtain to the section reserved for first-class passengers.

There were even fewer passengers in this section. It was almost empty. He preceded her to where he'd been sitting. The air hostess smiled indulgently and gave Alex a knowing look.

'Fasten up.' He leaned across, and

pulled at her safety belt.

His nearness was overwhelming and she felt the electricity of his touch as he stuck the fastener of the belt in the lock. Catrin buried her confusion.

'Thanks,' she managed.

Once they were airborne, the stewardess approached with two sparkling flutes of champagne. He took them both, gave her a wide smile, and handed one of them to Catrin.

'Here's to us!'

They looked at each other and Catrin found it was easy to smile despite the uncertainty of not knowing what he thought of her. Last night, he'd suggested that Toni was a flirt. Was he any better?

'This is luxury,' she said. 'More leg room, and a very personal service.'

He nodded.

'This route is generally good. In the holiday season, it's always full. I use this airline often. I sometimes get a forewarning about special offers and I book in advance whenever I can.'

'Always first class?' she couldn't help remarking.

'No, I fly economy most of the time, especially between London and Paris because it's such a short journey. If it's a longer flight, business or first class gives me the chance to do some work on the way.'

Although it was a five-hour flight, the time flew as they discussed books, films, favourite food, and hobbies. She found he enjoyed sailing and he discovered Catrin loved wandering around flea markets and antique shops.

When the announcement came to prepare for landing, he stood up and picked up his Barbour jacket from the adjoining seat.

'I need this, the temperature outside is definitely much cooler. I hope you have a jacket for when you land in London.'

She nodded.

'I put it on top of my bag.' She got up. He held out his hand and she took it. 'I'm going back to economy for the

133

final part of the journey to London.'

He smiled.

'I'm sure no-one will mind if you stay here — it's the same crew. But if it makes you feel better. We'll keep in touch, I hope. Is someone meeting you?'

'No, I'll catch the first available train back home. I've parked near the station. Do you live in Paris?' she couldn't help asking.

'I have a tiny one-room apartment, and I hope Anne will be at the airport to meet me, otherwise I'll take the fast train into the centre.'

She didn't want to ask who Anne was.

The flight attendant came to warn them they would be landing in a few minutes. Catrin walked back through the dividing curtain and looked at him before it fell back into place. The stewardess was talking to him. She blocked Catrin's view.

When she reached her seat, she belted up again and a few minutes later, they landed. The airport building was on the other side of the plane, so there was no chance of seeing him disappear into the tube-like connection and into the airport building.

After new passengers for London joined the plane, it took off again to its final destination a short time later. She had a brief period to think about the weekend.

Alex's unexpected arrival had changed everything. She ought not let that colour, or interfere, with her former intentions. She resolved to find out if there were any plans for building on Hazel's fields. She couldn't go on thinking about Alex Lorenzi in more personal terms if he was only after Hazel's land.

★   ★   ★

Back at work the following Monday, she used her coffee break to contact the local planning office.

'Have you a site number, or anything

else to help us to pinpoint your enquiry?' she was asked. Why are you enquiring if you aren't the owner and seeking building permission?'

Catrin only wanted to find out if Alex Lorenzi's name cropped up anywhere.

'The ground belongs to my aunt,' she explained. 'I just want to check the situation to make sure that she knows what's involved if someone buys her land.'

'Well, unless you can give me an official planning number or something similar, I'm afraid I can't help. Just telling me where the piece of land is, isn't enough information. If your aunt still owns the land, it isn't likely that someone else has planning permission. Someone else would need to own it before applying for official permission.' There was a short pause. 'Are you thinking of someone in particular, who might be applying?'

'There's an architect called Alex Lorenzi who may be a possibility. He owns a building firm and he knows my aunt.'

'Lorenzi? Yes, I know him but he hasn't applied for permission for anything in the area recently. I doubt if any architect would bother applying for building permission unless he had the site in his pocket.'

Catrin decided she'd get no further.

'Well, thank you anyway. If I do find any details. I'll get in touch again.'

'Yes, do that Miss . . . ?'

'Catrin, Catrin Watson. My number — '

'I have your telephone number on my display,' the woman told her.

Betrayed!

Catrin phoned Hazel in Corsica every couple of days and she seemed to be enjoying herself. She sounded much better and told Catrin enthusiastically about her various excursions with Anthony and Maria.

Catrin was busy as her plans for the special autumn exhibition were gradually coming together. Clearing her desk, she looked forward to a lazy weekend. As she was just about to leave the museum, the reception rang through to tell her someone was waiting for her in the entrance hall. Puzzled, she grabbed her things and hurried downstairs.

Her heart skipped a beat when she saw his tall figure pacing the hallway. She took a deep breath to be ready to face him. When he saw her, he came towards her, stopping abruptly when they actually met.

Her emerging smile died when she saw the expression on his lips. Her heart sank and she tried to control the feeling of disappointment.

His jaw clenched and his eyes narrowed. He cut short any preliminaries, thrust his hands deep into the pockets of his long coat, and assumed a cold expression.

'Why did you do it?'

It felt like there was a chill between them.

'Do what?'

'Phone the planning people and suggest that I had devious plans for Hazel's land.'

Her nerves tensed and her colour heightened.

'I didn't suggest any such thing. I just wanted to check if there were any plans. The woman asked if I had any particular name in mind and as you are the only architect that Hazel knows, I mentioned it. I didn't suggest you were doing anything illegal or underhand. I just wanted to find out if there were building plans. She didn't know and couldn't, or wouldn't, tell me.'

He stared at her, looking baffled and annoyed.

'Do you honestly think that I want to cheat Hazel,' he retorted in a cold sarcastic voice, 'and that that's the only reason I'm interested in her? To gain possession of her property?'

Her colour deepened and she swallowed hard as she looked at him. She couldn't find the right words fast enough.

His face was set, his mouth clamped tight and his eyes fixed.

'I misjudged you. I thought you were nice, but you're not. Underneath you're suspicious, distrustful, and unpleasant.'

She felt as if he'd struck her physically. She lifted her hand in protest while trying to organise in her mind what she should say. She could understand why he was angry.

'Alex, you are being unfair. Please try to understand, I only want to protect

Hazel. I know it sounds like I targeted you, but we only met recently and it seemed logical to check on things. Is it hard for you to understand that I wondered if you were getting Hazel's property for less than its worth? If you feel insulted, I apologise.'

The line of his mouth tightened even more.

'You've met me twice, and that is enough for you to think I want to do Hazel out of her property? Do you also believe that was why I invited her to Corsica? To soften her up?' He made as if to turn away.

She reached out to touch his arm. He immediately let it fall to his side and threw her a look as sharp as a knife. Before she could say anything else, he stared at her for a second or two, before he pulled her into his arms and kissed her in a way that robbed Catrin of her breath.

He held her at arm's length and she could see from his expression that devils had guided his action, and he already regretted his kiss. She wondered for a brief moment if he'd kiss her again.

He didn't. He let go and Catrin considered his angry expression.

He met her glance straight on and his eyes were like two cold black stones.

'I'll make the arrangements for Hazel to come home. If she thinks she can't manage it on her own, I'll find time to fetch her myself. You don't need to bother.'

He sounded so fierce she wondered how she could ever have thought that he was sympathetic and kind. He turned on his heel and headed towards the exit.

There were no words of farewell and Catrin understood why. He was furious. And she could see from his point of view he was justified. He hadn't denied that he was interested in Hazel's land, but Hazel had already said it was because he wanted to help her financially.

She stood silently watching him until

he disappeared through the revolving door.

The woman on the information desk had watched their exchange with interest. Catrin looked at her and she turned away to stack some brochures.

Pulling her coat tighter around herself, Catrin followed him outside. When she stood at the top of the curved entrance steps, he had already reached his silver-coloured, sleek car, parked on double lines further down the street.

There was a woman leaning against the front wing of the car. Catrin couldn't see her features clearly but she was slim, fashionably dressed, and with shoulder-length reddish hair.

When she saw Alex coming, she straightened, asked something, and he nodded abruptly. They got into the car, Alex on the driver's side, and drove off with the wheels spinning noisily.

Catrin could feel her throat closing up, and threatening tears blurred her vision. Why did she feel guilty and have a sense of loss? He was no-one special. She stood for a moment, considered the situation.

Something suddenly clicked in her brain — the knowledge that he was the most attractive, interesting man she'd ever met. That realisation twisted and turned inside her, because she'd given him reason to dislike her. She remembered how much she had enjoyed his company when she was on Corsica. She'd never felt so comfortable, so right, with anyone before. It was almost like finding a twin soul.

She couldn't turn back the clock. She should have asked more questions about his plans the day they met or even later on. It would have given him an opportunity to explain where he stood. Perhaps he, or Hazel, would then have shown her there was no necessity for sneaky enquiries.

Their first meeting in the field behind Hazel's cottage, when she thought he was trespassing, had influenced her and made her believe he was insensitive and uncaring. She had made up her mind, without knowing him properly, that he had hidden motives for everything he did.

His unexpected kiss had utterly confused her and deprived her of sensible reaction. Did he want to show her he knew she was attracted and wanted to demonstrate he didn't care? She almost felt ashamed that she had longed for more.

She walked towards her car, deep in thought. She wondered how he'd found out about her enquiries.

Wait. The woman in the planning office knew the name Lorenzi. Alex had taken over his father's company. They'd probably dealt with the local planning office for years and the woman had simply warned him someone was out to make trouble.

So much for client confidentiality — but what was the point in Catrin complaining? It was too late now. The damage was done.

She tried to think of a way to put

things right without making herself look like a fool, but nothing came to mind.

Always on Her Mind

Time marched on. Catrin's work kept her busy, although she thought about Alex constantly. She wished he understood her motives.

She spoke to Hazel a couple of times on the phone. Hazel sounded a lot better and she extended her visit to Corsica by a week because she was enjoying herself so much. Anthony and Maria were taking her on trips and they'd introduced her to many of their friends.

Catrin called at Hazel's cottage on her way to visiting her mother one weekend. Everything was OK, and the garden looked fine.

The next time they spoke she heard that Hazel was returning the following Sunday, so she spent that weekend weeding and tidying the garden. Catrin knew if Hazel returned and found everything in disarray, she would dump her suitcases and don her wellies.

She hadn't mentioned Alex's name to Hazel during their conversation, but Hazel told her he was coming to the island for the weekend and accompanying her back to London.

The female members of the museum's staff had set up what they called a birthday kitty. Instead of celebrating each other's birthdays in the office, they decided to pay in regularly to a kitty to finance a special trip once a year. So far, the trips had turned out to be a great success. The four girls chose in turn where to go and what to do.

This year Irene had suggested a trip to London with a visit to a show and an overnight stay. It meant increased contributions, but everyone looked forward to it. Irene had organised everything and they met up at the station on Saturday morning.

Catrin liked her fellow workers, and the 'girls' only' trip made it even more interesting and fun.

By the time they got to London, found the hotel, and dumped their bags, they just had time for a short shopping spree in Oxford Street before it was time to rush back to freshen up for the theatre.

Irene had booked tickets for a lesser-known musical, but it was a lucky choice. The cast was good, the storyline easy to follow and the music was light and bubbly. They left the theatre feeling happy and agreed to end the evening at a nearby pub.

The pub was busy but they grabbed a table in one of the corners, and Catrin and Irene fetched the first round. Background music and loud chatter filled the air. They were happy to quench their thirst and chat about shopping acquisitions, the musical, husbands and partners they'd left at home and their impressions of London so far.

Catrin joined in with the fun and was glad she'd come. She looked around and felt almost an electric shock when she spotted Alex sitting at a nearby table with the woman she thought he was with the last time he came to the museum. She had a fleeting moment to absorb the impact before he looked up and met her glance.

Was it her imagination, or did his expression tighten and his jaw stiffen? The girl at his side looked ridiculously young. She had the kind of alabaster skin that often went with red hair, and she was elegantly dressed.

Catrin couldn't decide what to do, then she dipped her chin in his direction. She thought he might ignore her but he replied with the briefest of nods in return. Catrin turned away, still slightly shocked to find him there. It was a million to one chance.

Irene looked at her.

'Something the matter? You look like you've seen a ghost.'

Catrin pulled herself together.

'No, not a ghost. Just someone I know. I'm just surprised, that's all. It's a fluke. He's sitting over there with his girlfriend.'

Irene looked around without knowing who she was looking for.

'Is he an ex of yours?' Irene took a sip of her drink and waited expectantly.

Catrin shook her head determinedly and fiddled with a beer mat.

'No, just an acquaintance.'

She reached for her glass and tried to concentrate. The others' chatter carried her along, even though she didn't join in or comment much. Taken aback and startled, her thoughts whirled and she wished she could pretend he was unimportant.

She kept her head facing forward and was glad that she didn't need to go to the bar for the next round. A short time later, the temptation was too much and she looked across. People blocked her view at first until she had a clear view of where he'd been. They were gone. Someone else was sitting at the table. At first Catrin felt relief but then it changed to disappointment. He wanted to avoid her.

The unexpected encounter filled Catrin's thoughts for most of the evening even though she appeared outwardly cheerful and in good spirits. Back at the hotel, she was sharing a room with Irene. By the time they returned to their rooms, they were all tired. Catrin lay in bed and stared into the darkness. She could soon hear Irene's steady breathing.

She wondered why Alex Lorenzi bothered her so much. Their last meeting wasn't encouraging, in any sense of the word. Why couldn't she just forget him? He must have brought Hazel back and put her on the train before going out with his girlfriend afterwards. It was none of her business.

Thumping the pillow and after much turning and twisting, she did eventually fall asleep but next morning she was still bothered. She would have caught an earlier train home if she was alone, because the pleasure had gone out of the weekend.

★　★　★

Back at work on Monday, she phoned Hazel in her lunch break.

'Oh, Catrin, I really enjoyed myself, it was just great. Anthony and Maria were so kind, and my cough has disappeared completely. I didn't get used to the heat, though, even after three weeks. I kept out of the sun as much as I could, but apart from that it was a wonderful break.'

'That's good.' Catrin paused. 'Alex brought you back?'

'Yes. He came on Friday and we travelled back together on Saturday. He offered to bring me all the way, but I told him that was silly. I promised I'd get a taxi from the station this end, and then he made sure I was on the right train. He had some important meeting in London on Monday, so it fitted into his plans.'

Catrin bit her lip. Alex's important meeting was with a redhead. She didn't ask if Hazel had seen Alex's girlfriend, or if the girlfriend had been with him on Corsica before flying with him and Hazel to London.

'Don't go overdoing things now that you're home again.'

Hazel laughed.

'I won't, and don't think that I didn't notice that you'd been here and done some weeding. Thanks for the things you put in the fridge, too — it saved me rushing out to the shop straightaway.'

'You're welcome.'

'Before I forget, I must tell you there's a new face behind the counter in the village shop, a niece of the Watsons. A widow with a little girl. She seems very nice and she has a friendly manner. The Watsons hope that, if she likes the shop, she might take it over permanently. There are still enough customers locally. The Watsons are worried that they'll have to close if they can't find a replacement.'

'Yes, I know they were worried. That would be a pity. I can't imagine the village without the shop.'

'The little girl is eight or nine, so she'll be able to go to the local school for a couple of years. They were here, trying it out, for a couple of days when I was away and they are now planning to spend the school holidays and see if they can fit in. At the moment they live on the edge of Bristol and the little girl's mother is getting worried because there's been a lot of trouble on their estate recently.'

'It's not easy for a single mum with a little girl.'

'I don't know how they'll manage for living space if they decide to stay. The Watsons only have a couple of rooms above the shop themselves and there is only a box-room-sized guest room. They'll need somewhere else if they stay permanently.'

Catrin laughed.

'Wait and see. Village life and town life is very different. She may find it boring and too quiet. She could come and stay with you, couldn't she?'

Hazel was silent for a second or two. She didn't comment, and Catrin wondered if she'd said the wrong thing. It was only a spur of the moment thought, but it wasn't such a bad idea. Hazel wouldn't be on her own all the time, there were several unused rooms in the cottage, and it would help Hazel financially.

It all depended on what the woman and the little girl were like. It would be a good solution for all of them, even if the young woman eventually moved out to a place of her own.

Catrin dropped the subject and told Hazel about her trip with her colleagues to London. She didn't mention that she'd seen Alex in the pub. She presumed Alex wasn't likely to mention it to Hazel either.

'It sounds like you had a good time,' Hazel commented. 'What about a boyfriend? Anyone new on the horizon?'

'No. I'm not searching for a partner, Hazel. I'm quite happy with my life. If I meet someone special, OK, but if not I definitely don't intend to settle for second best.

' I've seen too many friends rush into marriage with the wrong man just because the biological clock was ticking fast and they thought time was running out.'

'Quite right, love. You have a responsible job and you like it. It is different these days. Women are so independent.

'Your uncle was a lovely man and I still miss him very much,' she murmured. 'Do you know that I talk to his picture every day? Your dad was a good man, too. I hope you find someone like one of them. Dependant, reliable, loving, and true.'

She paused.

'When you have a spare weekend, come and see all the photos I took of Corsica. They'll definitely cheer me up in the depths of winter. Between you and me, though, I love my cottage and the village too much to ever imagine living anywhere else.'

Catrin promised to come soon. She'd phone first, to hear if Alex was likely to call. If so, she wouldn't bother. They chatted for a couple of minutes about the village and Catrin's job. Catrin could tell Hazel was full of beans again, but delighted to be back in her own cottage in the quiet comfort of the English countryside.

* * *

The conferences about the forthcoming special display of Phoenician pottery and lifestyle, due in the autumn, were going well. Several other museums were lending exhibits and a local archaeologist who specialised in that era of history had promised to help with the presentation, explanations and some lectures on the subject. They needed a video to present how the Phoenicians lived and existed. Catrin had finally tracked down a BBC documentary programme and was negotiating its use. She'd need help to set it up and position it effectively.

Catrin was pleased that the exhibition was taking shape so well. One afternoon there was a meeting in the director's office to iron out the details. After some points had been cleared and approved, Catrin happened to pick up a sheet of paper from a neighbouring pile by mistake. It was a proposal about adding a new wing to the museum. She handed it back to Bert with an apology.

'Is that general knowledge? I haven't heard any talk about an extension.'

Bert was a middle-aged member of the administration board.

'It's no secret, but not official yet. A person who owns a couple of industrial companies, and was born in the town, suddenly longs for local recognition. Someone told him that the art collection we have on show is very limited, and we have to store a lot of stuff in the cellar, because of the lack of space. He said he'd finance a new wing.'

'Good heavens! What a bit of luck.'

Bert smiled and his plump cheeks rounded into pink apples.

'Yes, it's nothing short of a godsend. The management committee haven't come down to earth yet. I have no idea what it will cost, but it wouldn't surprise me if it runs into millions. The donor doesn't seem to mind. I hope he doesn't change his mind when he hears how much.'

'And? Any definite ideas about what it will look like yet?'

'We are still at the planning stage. We just know how much space is available, and how much we want left around the new building after construction — that sort of thing.'

'So, an architect hasn't been chosen yet?'

'No, our donor demands an open competition. He fought his way up, and as long as they produce good designs, he wants to give less prominent architects a chance. He believes the architects at the top of the pile have already made their name on other projects and they'll be more expensive.

'They also often have a team of younger architects under them feeding them with the actual ideas. He wants to be on the panel that makes the final choice, although the board of trustees will make the preliminary choices. The design has to blend with the old building and carry our donor's name, but that's fair enough.'

Catrin was contemplative.

'Will you let me know when architects can apply, Bert? I know someone who might be interested. He's a young architect, and he has had some experience already, but I can imagine that something like this might be right up his street.'

Bert nodded.

'Will do. If you like, you can give me his business address. We're planning to make up a list of likely candidates and send all of them the information. Initially we intend to get in touch and ask them to give us an idea of what they'd suggest.

'We'll filter out the most likely candidates and then ask them to submit a proper design. Then the final panel will choose who gets the final commission to do it.'

'This goes over your desk?'

'Yes, the initial stages, but when Grenville and I have narrowed the field, the administrative board, our trustees, and our donator, will take over.'

Catrin floundered for a second or two.

'Please don't mention to my friend that I suggested his name.'

Bert stroked his chin.

'Whyever not? If he doesn't come up to scratch, that's it. I wouldn't choose him just to please you. It is too important for the museum.'

She nodded.

'I know that you'll be honest. It is only because we had a bit of a personal argument recently and he wouldn't want to be beholden. He's a good architect. I've seen some of his work in real life and pictures of others on his website. He deserves a chance.'

'Well, when I send him the general information, I could add a note that someone recommended him, without actually mentioning a name. It would be strange if I said I'd just picked up his name by chance. He'll probably still guess it was through you — unless he has done a lot of other work locally and thinks that is where I got the idea from.'

'Most of his work has been abroad — at least I think so, but I'm sure he's designed stuff in the UK, too. He isn't just an architect, he owns a small building company, so he knows the inside and out of the whole building process. I just thought it would be a wonderful opportunity for someone like him. Someone who is still climbing the ladder.'

Bert gathered the rest of his papers and bundled them into his battered attaché case.

'Well, give me his business address

and we'll see what happens. Perhaps I can find out more about him beforehand. My request would sound more casual if I can refer to other projects, although I still think he'll guess why we included him, if he knows that you work here.'

'He does. That would be great. I'll send you his details. You'll keep me in touch?'

'Of course.'

'I'm really pleased for the museum, Bert, and I'm sure that, as always, you'll do a wonderful job of pulling all the threads and making a strong rope to keep it all together.'

He laughed and lifted his hand in farewell as he left. Catrin collected her bits and pieces. She wondered if he would like what he saw on Alex's website. She'd check the address again as soon as she got back to her office and send it to Bert.

She found Alex's working address straightaway. His name was unusual enough to stand out from the rest.

The website included some pictures of items he'd designed, including a library in South Essex, and an administration building for a small town in Provence.

We Meet Again

Summer sped along. Catrin visited Hazel a couple of times and met the new woman in the shop. Her little girl was playing with some others in the back garden. The woman seemed to be coping well and was very friendly and pleasant.

The Watsons would be able to retire gradually into the background, which meant they'd have more freedom than they'd had for years. There was even tentative talk of them going on holiday.

One afternoon Catrin was sitting with Hazel on the terrace having tea.

'I've been thinking about what you suggested.'

'What do you mean?'

'About letting out rooms to that young woman and her little girl. I had them here to tea one Sunday and she loved the cottage and showed a lot of interest in the garden.

'The little girl is a gem, and told me her secret wish is to have a dog, but at the moment they haven't room for one in Bristol as her mummy is out working as a temporary clerk most days, and there is no-one else to look after a dog.'

Catrin nodded.

'And you think it will work? You won't get on one another's nerves?'

'I haven't suggested anything yet. I want to talk to her again when the little girl isn't around. I want to see how she feels before I commit myself to anything.

'I have enough room. At the moment they are squeezed together in the Watsons' box-room and they have to hang their clothes out in the shed.'

'Well, just remember that everyone needs their own space, and everyone needs to be private sometimes. You need your privacy as well as them. You'd have to share the kitchen and I know how much you love cooking. You do have enough spare rooms to give them both a bedroom of their own and turn another one into a sitting-room.'

'I know. I'll think about it carefully before I offer. It would be nice to have some company on a winter's night, though. Perhaps they'll only need somewhere to stay until they find somewhere permanent. Tell me what you've been doing. When are you going on holiday? Where are you going this year?'

'I'm down for the first weeks in September, but I haven't booked anything yet. I'd like to go to Tuscany and it won't be so hot at that time of the year. A friend of mine might join me, if she can get the same time off. We could rent a house together.'

'Why don't you go back to Corsica? You seemed to like it there. I'm sure Alex would help you to find somewhere to stay. Perhaps he'd even offer you his house if he doesn't need it himself.'

'No, I wouldn't want that.' Her reply was too sharp and too brusque. Catrin tried to soften the impression. 'It was kind of him to let me stay with you that time. He wanted to help you get over your bronchitis and if you were a seasoned air traveller you wouldn't have needed me at all.

'I don't want to intrude. We hardly know each other. I don't suppose he gets enough chances to go there as often as he wants as it is. I don't think he wants to let it out, he said so once.'

Hazel looked at her in surprise.

'I know you're not the type to intrude, and I think he knows that, too. He could suggest some place to stay, not necessarily in his house. I'm sure you could rent a house or a flat there. It is a beautiful island.'

Catrin picked up her cup and took a sip.

'Yes, it is. Have you seen Alex recently?'

'He hasn't been here since I got back, but he did phone the other day, to see how I was. It was very kind of him. It isn't as though we are related. I'm always surprised that he takes so much trouble.'

'That's because you are a nice person. You never complain about anything. Being with you is so easy.'

Hazel smiled.

'Go on with you! Flattery will get you anywhere. Want a piece of strawberry flan?'

★   ★   ★

Catrin met Bert in the corridor the following week. They smiled in passing then Bert remembered something and called her back.

'That architect laddie you mentioned? He's on the list of possible candidates.'

'Is he? That's good. How many are on the list?'

'Roughly twenty. There are a couple of better-known names, but quite a few, like your friend, are established but not top names yet. They now have a couple of weeks to submit some rough sketches and then it reaches the stage of choosing the final design.'

'Do they know the details now? How much space, and all the rest?'

'We sent them pictures of the proposed site, the present museum, and details about dimensions and the limit for costs. If they're sensible, some will pay a visit to look for themselves. If your friend does that, shall I let you know when he's here?'

She shook her head vigorously.

'No, it wouldn't look good for any employee to show partiality.'

He nodded.

'I'll keep you informed.'

As Catrin continued on her way, she wished that she could forget Alex. It was still far too easy to recall his features. Recently when out with a nice chap she met through a friend, she spent most of the evening comparing his attitude and appearance to Alex. It was ridiculous and it had to stop.

★ ★ ★

A fortnight later, she was coming down the stairs connecting the ground and first floors. She looked around the entrance hall. When she saw Alex standing there, she couldn't suppress a prickle of excitement.

Her step faltered for a fraction of a second and she gripped the bannister tightly. He had seen her, so there was no time to hide or go back upstairs. He stood waiting.

Her breath was suddenly uneven and her limbs unsteady, but she managed a hesitant smile when they met.

'Alex, what brings you here?'

Each time she saw him the pull she felt was stronger. That was something she did not understand at all, especially after their last meeting.

He seemed pleased with himself, and there was a small smile on his lips.

'I think you can guess. You suggested my name for the list of competitors for the new wing, didn't you?'

She shook her head.

'I have nothing to do with the interim

list you are on now.' She cleared her throat. 'I did mention your name to the man who is organising things when he made up the initial list of names, but any decision will not be down to me or my department. I just thought it might interest you, and as you are the only architect I know I mentioned your name.'

His dark eyes sparkled.

'I'm glad — that I'm the only architect you know. Otherwise, the competition would be even greater. I'm surprised you bothered at all, after our parting last time I saw you. I'm sorry for going over the top like that. Later on I have to admit I understood why you might be suspicious.' He hesitated before he continued. 'Oh, that wasn't the last time, was it? I saw you briefly in London.'

She coloured slightly and shrugged.

'I was there with friends for the weekend.'

'And I didn't want to interrupt. You seemed to be enjoying yourselves, and a stranger butting in might have dampened the atmosphere.'

She didn't comment.

'Are you here to look around the proposed site?'

'I visited one Saturday morning just after I received the first information. I'm here to hand in my rough designs.'

'I'm never here on Saturdays unless there's an emergency.'

'Lucky you. Sometimes I have to sacrifice my weekends because a prospective buyer is only available at the weekend. Look, once I've handed in my design shall we have a coffee in the cafeteria?'

She hesitated, but commonsense stepped in. She looked up at him and was conscious of his tall well-muscled body. Her memory recalled how he'd looked in shorts and casual polo shirt that weekend in Corsica. His face still looked tanned and healthy.

She pulled herself together and concentrated on sounding sensible.

'That would be nice, but it's not a

good idea. If people from the museum notice that we're chummy, they might think I'm trying to influence the result about who gets the commission. I've already told Bert that I want to keep my name out of the whole process, in case someone starts drawing the wrong conclusions. It's nothing personal.'

Catrin thought she saw momentary disappointment in his expression, but he replied quickly.

'Yes, of course. I can understand that. Pity, though. Perhaps another time, when this is all over?'

Catrin didn't think it was likely. They wouldn't meet in the museum unless his bid was successful. Even then, she wasn't likely to see much of him. He would be dealing with a completely different group of people. She'd avoid meeting him at Hazel's if she could. He had a girlfriend already, after all.

'Yes, perhaps. You'd better carry on and hand your design in to Bert. How do you feel about your chances?'

He smiled and her heart skipped a beat.

'I'm happy with my design and I think it would look good, but you can never be certain. There's always fierce competition. Architects all need to make a living and make a name for themselves.'

'Well, I wish you luck. I'm sure that you have an impressive design, and I hope it's better than any of the others.'

He nodded.

'Considering that the only building of mine that you've ever seen is my house on Corsica, I'll take that as a great compliment. Perhaps we'll meet at Hazel's one day soon?'

'Perhaps, who knows? Nice to see you, Alex, and I'm glad we're not at loggerheads any more. I didn't mean any harm by making enquiries at the planning office, honestly.'

He nodded but remained silent. He leaned forward and kissed her cheek.

Her colour heightened.

'What was that for?'

'Just my way of saying thanks — and because I feel like it.' He raised the long tube containing his plan in a gesture of farewell, turned and strode towards the stairs with long, confident steps.

Catrin turned in the opposite direction towards the tourist shop. She actually needed to go in the same direction he was going, to talk to someone about rearranging the space for children's learning and playing, but she wanted to give him time to disappear.

The strange surge of affection she felt for him frightened her. She had never felt anything like it before with any other man she'd ever met.

Close Companions

Weeks later, Catrin was leaving a meeting in Bert's office when he stalled her.

'I suppose you know that your friend won the commission?' he said, smiling.

The breath caught in her throat and she hoped she didn't look like a landed fish.

'No, I didn't. That's good.'

'Yes, and I must admit it is a very interesting and impressive design. It wasn't easy to find the right balance between connecting the old and the new. He's obviously given a lot of thought to the surroundings and the impending impact. Have you seen his plans?'

'No. As I told you, we're not close friends.'

'I like him. He's plain-speaking, intelligent and very knowledgable. The new wing will cover three thousand square metres and has a slightly flattened dome.'

Catrin nodded.

'The connection from the main building will be through traditional-looking arches. Their supporting pillars will frame the entrance doors to the new wing. The whole area is open up to roof level. It will have a first-floor gallery on the southern side, big enough for smaller special exhibitions, and a mezzanine cafeteria. The roof itself will have a system of solar thermal collectors to reduce our running costs. The internal walls will be in neutral tones with ceramic tiles, stonework, and some strips of muted coloured glass.

'It is going to be an innovative building with modern technology that won't compete with the old building for attention. If I remember rightly, external slanting strips of rusted iron merge the old with the new. There'll be no immediate feeling that the old building has ended and the new is beginning.

'On the far side of the room, floor-length windows will integrate the view of what remains of the garden, and provide light on that side of the room. I'm very impressed, and delighted that the committee have chosen this particular design.'

'It sounds good,' Catrin admitted. 'I haven't seen very much of what Alex has designed, but I have seen some of the buildings on his website, and they look impressive. The committee have made a good choice.'

'When all the details are figured out and the actual work can begin, he says he thinks it will take roughly a year, perhaps a little longer to complete.'

He paused.

'I'll be arranging a small get-together sometime soon so that everyone can take a look at what's planned. The trust committee will be there, the press and we'll invite all the museum employees. Alex Lorenzi, too, of course, so you'll be able to judge yourself what you think of it, and have a chat to your friend at the same time.'

He looked at his watch.

'I must get on. I have a meeting in ten minutes with a firm about the air conditioning on the second floor. One of the curators thinks it isn't working properly and that would be a problem for our art collection there. We need to be very careful about temperatures on that floor.'

She nodded.

'And I'm scheduled to talk to my counterpart in Cardiff to find out which items they'll lend us for the autumn show.'

As Catrin walked on she felt a multitude of conflicting emotions. She was exultant for Alex that he'd won the commission and looked forward to seeing him again, but half in anticipation and half in dread, because she wasn't sure if she could control how she felt about him any more.

She would send him an e-mail offering congratulations. She had his telephone number from the time he rang up about Hazel's trip, but an e-mail to his website address would suffice.

★ ★ ★

The room was already full when she arrived. People were standing around with glasses of wine and there was loud chatter among her fellow workers. The museum had officially closed for the day and this get-together was just to show everyone the plans for the new wing. The design was pinned on a board and people crowded around it.

Catrin picked up a glass from one of the trays and asked Bert's secretary if she could help. Irene shook her head and gestured to the bottle in her hand.

'I'm just offering refills as I go around. I don't think Bert wants it to be a party — that's why there are no nibbles.'

Catrin looked around.

'I expect most people won't hang

182

around long. Holding it straight after working hours was a good idea. People want to know what's happening but I don't think that they want to discuss any details for too long.'

Irene nodded.

'The architect is over there. I haven't heard a lot of criticism from anyone. I think that if the new extension looks like the plans, people will be very satisfied. I like it. It's modern without going to extremes.'

Someone held out his glass and Irene busied herself with filling it.

Catrin moved on.

She spotted Alex as soon as she entered. He was taller than most of the men present. He was dressed in black, which made him stand out even more.

He was nodding at someone in front of him and his expression lightened. Catrin took a deep breath and just decided it was time to go across and say hello, when she noticed the woman with the red hair standing at his side. Her steps faltered for a moment and a feeling of regret flooded her.

Just then, he looked up and their eyes met. He beckoned her over. She paused for a moment, burying her disappointment. She reasoned that it was obvious he'd want his girlfriend to be with him on an occasion like this.

'Catrin!' He smiled. 'So, as you know, I made it to the top of the list!'

'Yes, and you deserve it. I just had a quick look at your design, and I agree wholeheartedly with the committee's choice.'

His expression sent her pulses racing.

'Thanks! As you were instrumental in mentioning my name in the first place, I feel very indebted. Thank you for the e-mail, by the way.'

'Did you get it? Good!'

He turned to the redhead in a very smart bottle-green costume at his side. The collar and cuffs had a narrow black edging, and the jacket had attractive black buttons. The flattering skirt barely skimmed the top of her knees.

Catrin didn't have many designer

items in her wardrobe, but she recognised one when she saw it. The woman's costume was upmarket and chic. Catrin's grey skirt and crisp white blouse couldn't compete — but what did it matter?

'I don't think you've met Anne, have you?'

'No. Pleased to meet you.'

Catrin offered her a smile and her hand. She hoped she looked more affable than she felt.

'Alex told me that you gave the committee his name,' she said, in a soft French accent, as she shook Catrin's hand. 'It was very helpful.'

Catrin gripped her glass tighter and told herself there was no reason for her to be unfriendly or hostile in any way. The only problem she had with this woman was the fact that she had a very attractive and intelligent boyfriend.

Catrin wished she could change places with her.

'His design won without any help from me,' Catrin hastened to say.

'Nothing I did made any difference to the final decision.'

'But I wouldn't have even heard about it without you.' Alex smiled. 'I'm grateful to two special women. Anne here keeps me on my toes and you helped by putting my name forward.'

He threw his arm round Anne's shoulder. Anne blushed slightly and looked at him with an expression close to awe.

'She's irreplaceable.'

Catrin nodded and cleared her throat.

'I'm sure she is.' She was almost glad when one of the curators interrupted to ask him a question about his design.

Alex shrugged imperceptibly in her direction and followed the curator towards the plans to answer his query. Anne gave her a parting look and automatically trailed after him.

Catrin was free to finish her drink quickly, and after chatting with some of her colleagues, she hurried back to her office, grabbed her things and hastened downstairs, out into the fresh air.

She breathed deeply and was glad to be on her own. Straightening her shoulders, she pretended she didn't care that he had an attractive redhead who clearly adored him.

She strode off determinedly to her car and a few minutes later, she pulled out into the evening traffic.

* * *

Catrin kept herself busy cleaning the inside of the oven — a task she disliked. It didn't distract her thoughts long enough. Finally, fed up with her own ridiculous thoughts, she phoned Brian.

After the preliminaries, she asked if they could meet up for a drink and a chat at the weekend. It was so out of character that Brian was lost for words for a moment.

'Only if you have time, of course,' Catrin added quickly.

He was clearly surprised, but delighted.

'I have all the time in the world for you! What about tomorrow evening? We could go dancing, for a meal, or the pictures and a meal afterwards.'

'Whatever you like. Where shall we meet?'

'I'll pick you up and we'll go to the latest thriller, or would you like something else?'

'No, that's fine. What time?'

'Six?'

'Right, I'll be ready and waiting.'

When she put the receiver down, she knew she was only looking for an excuse to fill the empty hours and tell herself that Alex Lorenzi wasn't the only one who would be enjoying themselves this weekend.

* * *

Aunt Hazel phoned to tell her that she had decided to rent a couple of rooms to the village's prospective shopkeeper.

'She seems to be a very sensible girl, and her daughter is well brought-up.

They are staying with me during the summer holidays and then I'll have an idea whether we do get along or not. We've agreed to share the evening meal, but each of us will sort out the rest of the mealtimes. She'll keep her rooms clean and tidy and help with the kitchen.'

'It sounds OK. In fact, it's a good idea. You'll only know whether you get on if you live with them for a while.'

'That's what I thought, too. If I find it doesn't suit me, I don't need to continue the arrangement later. It is important for her and the little girl, too, of course.'

'I can see the advantages and the disadvantages for you both.'

'So can I. Even if we do get on, there is a possibility that she might want to go elsewhere later on.'

'That's true.'

'Whenever you have a free weekend between now and the end of the holidays come and meet her. She's busy in the shop until two o'clock on Saturday, but you'll see her if you come at teatime. I think Alex quite likes her. Anyway, that's what he said.'

'Alex? Have you seen him?'

'Yes, he called in on his way back from the reception at your museum that day. It was good of you to mention him to the right people. He was proud that he won the commission and he said he'd spoken to you briefly.'

'Yes, I didn't stay very long. He was the centre of interest. I just proposed him to a colleague initially — the rest had nothing to do with me.'

'Well, getting his name mentioned in the right quarters is already a very useful step, isn't it?'

'Perhaps, but a very small one. His design won the commission because it's good.

'That had absolutely nothing to do with me. I didn't know what his design was like until I saw it on display. It's quite spectacular and I like it. Did he show it to you?'

'No, I think his drawings were out in the car. He didn't have much time. He was on his way back to London. He just popped in for a cup of tea and to see how I was.'

Catrin hesitated.

'Was Anne with him?'

'Anne? Who's Anne? No-one was with him. Is she a new girlfriend?'

Hazel paused for a second.

'Oh, yes — I remember the name now. There was an Anne with him on the flight between Paris and London — the day Alex brought me back from Corsica. She was sitting somewhere else on the plane. We only met briefly. I teased Alex about his girlfriend and he laughed it off.

'After we were through passport control and had collected our luggage, the two of them spoke for a moment or two, then he pecked her cheek and she picked up her bag. She waved in my direction and left. Do you think she's someone special?'

Catrin shrugged.

'She was with him at the reception in the museum.'

'Was she? Then they must be close. She's very attractive, isn't she? I like redheads, they're unusual, and somehow they always stand out in a crowd. In her case, I don't think the colour comes from a bottle either. She has very pale skin and a sprinkling of freckles. That's typical for redheads. Very smart, very slim, very striking.'

'Yes, I agree. She is very attractive,' Catrin agreed with a lump in her throat.

'What about you? Any romance in the air?'

'No. Nothing special to report.' Catrin changed the direction of the conversation. 'I'll phone before I come. I'm due to pay Mum a visit soon, so perhaps I'll call in on the way there, or on the way back.'

'Do that, love. Look forward to seeing you. Take care!'

'You, too. See you soon.'

⋆   ⋆   ⋆

Catrin did drop in one Saturday, and she liked Monica and her daughter.

They were clearly pleased to be living in the country. Monica liked the job in the shop and her daughter had already made friends with some of the children of her own age who were living in the village.

Hazel said she was an honest, hardworking young woman who'd had to cope with lots of problems since her husband died, and she hoped she could make a new start in surroundings that were good for her and her daughter.

Monica was interested in gardening, and that was a big plus in Hazel's eyes. Monica had given up gardening in her last house, because vandals always came along and wrecked everything.

'It's nice to have a bit of company around the house again, too.'

'And the little girl? Not too much noise or palaver?'

'No, she's a bright little thing, but polite and biddable.'

'Good, so everything is working out so far?'

'Yes, fine. Monica is even thinking of buying a small car if she stays permanently. Then she'll be more mobile in her leisure time.

'Let's have a cup of tea before you set off again. You're staying with your mum this weekend?'

'Yes, I haven't seen her for a while and David's baby is one year old tomorrow, so it's birthday time.'

Devastating Accusations

Several days later, when summer was making real inroads at last, Catrin was surprised to get a phone call from the planning office. The woman explained her name was Wallace, and that they'd spoken before.

'I don't usually get in touch with anyone who makes casual enquiries, but as I learned from Mr Lorenzi that our last conversation had caused a lot of friction, I thought it is only fair to tell you about the present position.'

'That's kind of you,' Catrin could only murmur, greatly surprised. 'Are there any new developments?'

'Yes, there are now enquiries about whether the whole site would be suitable for building, and how long planning permission will take if it is.

'Mr Lorenzi is a regular visitor to these offices and we all know him. He's been coming here ever since he started working with his father and he knows as much about the rules and regulations as anyone who works in this office. I don't want to cause any more trouble between you.' She laughed softly.

Catrin swallowed hard.

'That's thoughtful of you. Can you tell me who has applied?'

'No, I'm not allowed to mention names. But I can say there are two parties involved.'

'Is the site suitable for building?'

She hesitated on the other end of the telephone.

'This is completely unofficial — but yes. Things are still at the initial stage, of course. Just enquiries. Official permission must be acquired, local protection laws observed, geological problems sorted out, just like any site that comes up for building purposes. And archaeological finds in this area have often halted, or ended prospective building plans.'

'Is Mr Lorenzi one of the interested parties?'

There was silence on the other end of the line.

'I'm sorry, I can't confirm or deny that. I'm already overstepping the limits in contacting you at all and I must ask you not to mention my name. It could cost me my job.'

Catrin backed off.

'No, of course. You have my word. Thank you for telling me as much as you have. I'll do my best to make any further enquiries as discreetly as I can and without mentioning you or your department in any way.'

'Good! I hope you'll find out what you need to know. Bye!'

'Bye!' Catrin replaced the receiver with a sinking heart.

She thought about it for a couple of days, wondering what to do. In the end, she decided to talk to Hazel to find out what, if anything, she knew about it all.

She got to the cottage to find Hazel in the garden tying up some delphiniums. She looked up when she heard the gate opening.

'Catrin! What a surprise. I didn't expect to see you again so soon.'

Catrin kissed her cheek, smiled, and glanced around the garden. It was a blaze of flowers. Hazel's vegetable garden was further down the garden, hidden behind arched rose bushes and neatly cut hedges. Hazel began to pull off her gardening gloves.

'I'll put the kettle on and make us a cup of tea.'

'No, carry on. I'll make the tea and bring it out.'

Hazel didn't argue and straightened the battered straw hat on her head before she concentrated on the task in hand.

'Do that. I'll look forward to a break in a minute or so.'

A few minutes later Catrin returned with the tray of crockery, a teapot under a tea cosy and some biscuits from the biscuit barrel. She arranged the things on the wrought-iron round table. She remembered how she had painted it for Hazel last summer. It was a day like this with not a cloud in the sky.

Hazel ambled across, took off her gloves and slapped them once or twice. She sat down and sighed.

'Just what I need. Pour me a cup, love.'

Catrin did as requested, and she then picked up her own cup.

Hazel looked across the table and studied her for a moment or two.

'What's up? It isn't like you to turn up without any kind of warning. Is something wrong?'

Not knowing where to begin, Catrin struggled to find the right words.

'Not really, but I do have a reason. It's about you, about this cottage and about your fields.'

'Yes, and . . . ?'

'I think someone may be hoping you'll sell them cheaply.'

Hazel didn't seem surprised.

'Why do you think that?'

'I've been checking up and apparently there are two parties interested in your land. There's even talk of building.'

Hazel took a big sip of tea and put the cup down in the saucer. It rattled as she did so.

'And do you know who these 'two parties' are?'

'No, but I suspect someone.'

'Who?'

Catrin hesitated, but she'd gone too far to stop now.

'Alex. I'm afraid he might persuade you to do something that might not be in your own interests.'

Hazel stiffened.

'Catrin, you know that I love you. I never thought that you'd upset me. I've known Alex all his life! Alex is not like that.'

'But he's an architect! Business is business, Hazel. Don't you think it is possible that he might try to take advantage?'

Hazel's face reddened.

'No, I don't! Before you go any further, I'm perfectly aware about the negotiations for the fields. Billy Rainer asked me months ago if there was any chance of him buying the ones he uses.

'I asked Alex what he thought about it. Alex said he'd take the other one behind the cottage and build houses there. He even made quick sketches of what a couple of houses in the field would look like. I like the idea. What use are the fields to me any more? I'm not a farmer and I'm the last of my family.'

Catrin was lost for words.

'I like the idea of new families,' Hazel continued. 'It'll help to keep the village alive. I'm not getting any younger and when something happens to me the fields will be sold off anyway, so I'm glad to have a say in things now, when I'm still around.'

Catrin frowned.

'And Alex didn't push you? He has nothing to do with your final decision?'

'Of course not. I trust him implicitly.'

Catrin straightened and stared unseeingly ahead of her, just listening.

'Things are still at the discussion stage,' Hazel went on. 'Billy is a farmer through and through. He'd never want to use the land for building and his son wants to take over the farm when his dad retires. The field behind the house isn't much use for farming, and I'm going to sell it to Alex if he wants it. I know he'll do his best for himself, and for me.'

Catrin fidgeted on her chair. There were tears threatening at the back of her eyes. Hazel had never decided anything so important without talking to her about it beforehand. She felt shut out.

'It's up to you, of course,' she said. 'Just think carefully about everything before you come to your final decision.'

Hazel clucked her tongue and her face reddened.

'I see you have a bee in your bonnet. I think you misunderstand Alex's motives. What's he ever done to upset you?'

'Nothing. Nothing at all. I just want

you to understand that once you sell the fields, you won't have any say in what happens to them after that. What about the coppice?'

'I'm going to give that to some local nature reserve group. Monica said she'll help me find some information about that.'

Catrin was slightly shocked, because the longer she talked to Hazel, the more she felt locked out of all her decision-making.

'Monica? Monica knows all about this?'

Hazel noticed.

'Now don't get all upset. I intended to talk to you about it. The business about the coppice just slipped out when I was talking to Monica this week. We were watching a TV programme about endangered species and it just tumbled out.'

Catrin stood up and tried a weak smile before she grabbed her bag from the back of the chair.

'It's up to you, and I understand

and respect that. It's just a bit of a surprise and I need to process it. I'll phone in a day or two. I'm sure you'll do the right thing. If I can help in any way just tell me.' She walked swiftly away along the terrace and turned around the corner.

Catrin heard Hazel calling her name, but she hurried down the path and into her car. The gravel shot off to the side of the wheels as she drove away.

Rubbing her eyes to prevent advancing tears, she concentrated on the road ahead. She was more upset about the fact that Hazel hadn't consulted with her, than about the actual decisions. For the first time, Catrin felt shut out of Hazel's life.

$\star$ $\star$ $\star$

Two days later, an unexpected phone call at work sent Catrin winging her way to the hospital. When she got there and found out where she could find Hazel, she didn't wait for the lift but raced up the stairwell as if the hounds of hell were at her heels. By the time she reached the third floor she was out of breath.

There was the typical faint smell of disinfectant in the air and ahead of her the long corridor with its shiny floor stretched endlessly.

Catrin spotted Alex's tall figure before he saw her. He was pacing up and down like a tiger in a cage. He was facing away from her at present and running his hand through his hair impatiently. She steadied her thoughts and caught her breath.

The sounds of her heels made him turn around. His face was grim, and the closer she got, the better Catrin saw that his mouth was a thin line and his tanned skin was stretched taut over his cheekbones.

'How is she?' Catrin's voice was quiet and anxious.

Fearful images had been growing in her mind all the way to the hospital. Catrin still had haunting memories of how her father had died so suddenly before he even reached the hospital. She couldn't bear to think she might lose Hazel, too.

'She's OK. They just think it was the result of extremely high or low blood pressure. They intend to keep her under observation for twenty-four hours.'

His reply was matter-of-fact but the expression on his face wasn't. He looked strained and angry.

Catrin found she longed to reach up and touch his cheek but, of course, she didn't. She was relieved that Hazel wasn't in any immediate danger. It looked like things were not as bad as she feared.

Her relief was short-lived.

'Monica phoned me at work,' she told him. 'She found my number in Hazel's address book. I can't believe it. I called in last weekend and she was OK. What happened? I know she has wonky blood pressure but the doctor prescribed tablets for that.'

He shrugged and frowned, his dark

eyes were level under straight drawn brows.

'I don't know exactly what happened. Although it's not surprising, is it? She takes on too much in that darned garden, has to carry heavy shopping baskets, and doesn't always look after herself properly.

'She often joked that she'd forgotten to take her tablets and she insisted it didn't make the slightest difference if she did or not. I thought you were very close and were keeping an eye on her.'

Was it her imagination or was there reproach in his tone?

She felt forced into the defensive.

'Hazel never wanted to discuss her blood pressure with me. I knew that she needed medication and I told her more than once she had to remember to take her tablets. I presumed she was sensible and took what the doctor prescribed.

'That bronchitis knocked her back recently, but I thought that her holiday on Corsica had cleared it up. In fact, I didn't worry so much about her being alone in the cottage any more, because Monica was living with her. She did mention she was tired now and then, but even my mother says that and she's younger than Hazel.'

'Being tired doesn't mean you end up in hospital. I think it is more likely due to all this fuss about selling or not selling the fields, and your stupid reaction to it.'

His remark upset her but she didn't show it. Nervously she bit her lip.

'I didn't know about all the plans until she told me. I was surprised, of course, and I'm honest enough to admit I felt shut out, but Hazel seemed happy with what was going on and I told her it was none of my business. I found that even Monica knew more about it than I did.'

'So you played the offended niece when you heard the details? Didn't you stop to think that it would upset Hazel no end?'

'What do you mean? I didn't intend to upset her! Are you suggesting that's what caused all this? Admittedly, I was very surprised when she told me about the developments, but that was because she hadn't mentioned it before and everyone else seemed to know what was going on.'

'So you played the injured diva?'

'No! It was just the surprise of hearing about everything so suddenly. I needed time to think about what she'd told me, before making the wrong kind of remarks.'

'How noble! It's strange how the world is full of good intentions.'

She was quietly furious but she didn't intend to make a scene. She wanted to ignore him. She didn't need Alex to make her feel guiltier than she did already.

'How did you find out that Hazel was ill and had been taken to hospital?' she asked.

'I had an appointment with the planning office. I called at the cottage afterwards and met Monica. She told me she'd called the doctor when she found Hazel collapsed. The ambulance had just left.'

'Can . . . can I see her?'

There was an edge to his voice as he answered.

'She's had some extra tests and they are now making her comfortable in the ward at the end of the corridor. She's on a drip, but she's beginning to feel better already.'

His words should have calmed her but they didn't. She couldn't help the exasperation in her voice as she recalled her last conversation with Hazel.

'I wish no-one had ever mentioned the fields or any of the rest now.'

She hoped for a few consoling words but was disappointed.

He shifted his weight and viewed her with direct, accusing eyes.

'No use crying over spilt milk, but since you mention it, I don't think your attitude did her any good — especially after you bolted like a spoilt child. She told me about it. You seem to believe I was trying to do her out of a fair price for the land.'

He shook his head, looking baffled.

'Were you worried that Hazel was about to give away what you thought might be yours? Was that the reason you dashed off and left her feeling miserable? She thinks of you as the daughter she never had.

'Just remember that Hazel is entitled to make her own decisions, even if you don't agree with what she decides. She is not senile. She chose what was best for herself and she made sensible decisions. If you'd kept your mouth shut it would have been better all round and she wouldn't be in hospital today.' His lips were thin lines and his gaze was angry.

Catrin stiffened with shock. His remarks and the caustic tone of his voice made her flush and then she went white as a sheet as his words sunk in.

'I beg your pardon? Are you accusing me of loving Hazel only for what she owns?'

She couldn't believe he was being so

spiteful, with Hazel lying in a hospital bed just a few doors away.

A cold knot formed in her stomach when she listened to him.

His voice was quiet, but held an undertone of contempt, as he continued.

'Before you started to pry and meddle your aunt was living a quiet, comfortable, simple existence. True, she couldn't afford much in the way of luxury, but she managed. If she sells the fields, she can spend the rest of her life in security and with enough money for whatever she wants. She's a strong independent, fighting character.

'You came along and made up your mind to oppose any sale, and you didn't worry about what was best for Hazel. Do you think she didn't notice that? I bet you she didn't want to tell you because she knew you'd argue. If you had a bit of sense in your head, you'd realise how much she likes the idea of financial independence. She is not foolish or irrational.'

Catrin flinched and felt ice spreading through her limbs. Her mouth tightened and stiffened as she looked up into his familiar face and then a slight tremor touched her stiff lips. He made her sound like an uncaring, ruthless female.

Her breath was shallow and her senses drugged. He was the man she'd coveted all her life and it was unbearable for her to listen with rising dismay to his barbed and hurtful words.

'So that means I'm to blame for today?'

She took a deep breath and tried to steady her voice.

'I love Hazel. I'd do anything — anything at all — to turn back the clock and find her well and happy in her cottage. I never wanted to upset her, that's the last thing I'd ever do. It was just a bit of a shock to hear about her plans.

'Of course she has the right to do what she wants. Do you think it was wrong of me to tell her to be careful in case someone took advantage of her?'

The expression on his face didn't change and she decided there was no point in carrying on.

'Excuse me. I'm going to find someone who can tell me what's happening.'

She brushed past him and hoped he didn't see the tears in her eyes. On the other hand, what did it matter? He didn't care whether he hurt her or not.

★ ★ ★

Alex's expression tightened and his dark eyebrows drew into a frown. His jaw clenched but he remained silent. Her expression reminded him of a whipped dog and he hated himself.

He watched her as she hurried away down the corridor. Something inside him snapped, but it was too late.

He lifted his hand in a vague restraining motion and then ran it through his hair instead.

He stared after her as she disappeared around the corner. His mouth tightened and his expression darkened before he finally turned away to get out of the antiseptic atmosphere that he hated so much, away from memories of hospitals that he loathed.

He turned away from the realisation that his hasty words had wilfully destroyed something between them that was infinitely important.

He hoped to goodness he could put it right again, sometime, somehow.

Life-changing Decisions

Catrin waited outside the department for a few minutes. She needed to compose herself, forget his remarks, and face Hazel. After a few minutes she lifted her chin and pushed the door open.

Hazel was lying in one of the beds near the door. A nurse looked up and when Catrin pointed towards Hazel, she nodded and went back to attending to another patient.

Catrin bent down, kissed Hazel's cheek and gave her a quick hug, being careful not to disturb the drip attached to her arm.

Hazel smiled weakly at her niece.

'Don't you dare cry! That's enough of that, Catrin — I'm not going to die.'

Catrin was glad she felt under control again, though her voice had a tremor to it.

'Can I have that in writing, please? Oh, Hazel! How do you feel? I wish I I'd been there to help.'

'I feel much better. I don't remember what happened. Apparently, my blood pressure was completely skew-whiff. I feel a bit of a fraud now but they want to check me properly before I can go home.'

'What happened exactly?'

'I didn't notice anything was wrong. I thought it was just indigestion at first, but it got worse and I felt very dizzy. When I tried to get up, I couldn't. I just fainted away. Monica heard the rumpus and came upstairs. She called the doctor and he called the ambulance service. The rest is history.'

Catrin could see that her aunt was feeling OK. That reassured her a little, and she relaxed.

'Did you forget your tablets? You know how important they are.'

Hazel gave her a sheepish look.

'I know. I'll take more care from now on. The doctor said it probably wouldn't have happened if I'd taken my medication like he'd prescribed.'

'I won't stay long now because you are supposed to be resting. I'll come later, promise! Do you need anything?'

Hazel nodded.

'I already have a packed suitcase on the bottom of my wardrobe. I put everything I'd need for a hospital stay in there — because I knew no-one else would find things if something happened unexpectedly. I hope I can go home tomorrow.'

Catrin gave Hazel another brief kiss.

'I'll find it. I'm glad you're feeling a little better. You'll feel better still in a while, I'm sure. Rest now and we'll have a longer chat next time I come.'

Hazel stroked the back of Catrin's hand.

'I'll try. Sorry to have caused all this trouble! I wish I'd told you about the fields earlier. I don't know why I didn't. Things moved so fast when the ball started to roll.

'I wanted to phone a couple of times,

but something or other always got in the way. I tried once but you weren't at home. When I thought about it later, it was bedtime.'

Catrin felt the tears welling again.

'Don't be silly, Hazel! It's OK. You are doing the right thing. I'm so glad Monica found you. I dread to think what might have happened if you'd been on your own. I'll see you later!'

'Oh, will you bring my library book — by the side of my bed?'

Catrin nodded.

'And Catrin? You should know that you and Alex share everything if something should happen to me. I sorted it out with Johnson and Baker in the high street years ago.

'When I first made my will, I left it to your dad and Alex because I thought they were the best people to decide what to do with the cottage and the land. I changed it to you and Alex when your dad died. You are the only people I trust implicitly. Off you go, and don't worry, I'm fine!'

Catrin knew this wasn't the time or the place to talk about business. She smiled and nodded. She waved as she reached the door and Hazel waved back.

Catrin walked out slowly through the swing doors. Even if Alex felt she was responsible for Hazel's breakdown, Hazel loved her enough to entrust her with what she prized most in this life. That helped.

The corridor was empty, and Catrin's mind whirled. The lift was busy, so she headed for the stairwell. At the turn of each storey, a window looked out over the entrance area. Glancing down, Catrin picked out Alex's silver convertible in the parking lot.

He was leaning against the bodywork, looking at his watch and waiting. She wondered why, but it didn't matter any more. She knew what he thought of her. She faced the sickening inevitability that he didn't like her.

She exited through a side entrance and took a roundabout route to where she'd parked her car not far from the hospital.

She drove back to Hazel's cottage and looked for the suitcase and the book then walked up to the shop and talked to Monica. They arranged to visit Hazel together later, after the shop closed. Monica could leave her daughter with her uncle and aunt for an hour or two.

The tests hadn't shown anything very serious or life threatening, but her blood pressure did need controlling. Hazel was frightened enough to say she'd follow the doctor's orders from now on. Hazel told Catrin that Alex promised he would take her home before he left for London.

'If they keep me in longer I'll take a taxi, so don't worry. You can't neglect your work because of me.'

Catrin nodded but didn't comment.

★ ★ ★

Catrin rang the cottage next morning and Hazel was back home. Monica had already promised to keep a close eye on her.

Catrin was glad to be busy at work. It left her little time to think about other things during the day. During the night, it was different. She couldn't sleep. Her thoughts circled around what Alex had said.

She tried running, exercising at the local gym, meeting friends, visiting her mother or Hazel at the weekend. Nothing helped very much. She kept thinking about Alex and how he blamed her for everything.

She clung determinedly to the belief she hadn't acted selfishly in trying to find out what was happening to the fields.

She struggled through days of aching misery and wondered if her life would ever be normal again. She had to concentrate on the fact that until she met Alex, she'd been perfectly happy and had a job she really liked and did well. He'd turned her world upside down in a very short time.

When she told her friend Gloria

about what had happened, she sympa-
thised.

'Just forget him,' she said angrily at
the end of their conversation. Catrin
nodded. Most of what Gloria said made
sense, apart from the part about
forgetting him. That was easier said
than done.

Chatting to Bert one day, he
mentioned that work on the new wing
was starting in October. On reflection,
she decided that it would be a good
time to re-evaluate her life. She hoped
that she could then move ahead; forget
him.

The new exhibition was opening in
September. Monica was living happily
with Hazel so she didn't need to worry
about her so much any more. Her
mother was fine and no matter where
she moved, her visits to Hazel or her
mother would go on, even if the journey
to see them took longer. She started to
check professional magazines for a new
job.

When she next phoned Hazel she was

glad to hear how bouncy her aunt sounded.

'I've finally decided to sell the fields, Catrin. Alex says he has too much on his plate at present to think about designing houses, but he'll get round to it as soon as he can. He suggests family houses with children. Ones that are not too expensive, individual and yet simple in design.

'Young families with children will revive village life, keep the primary school open, and force the council into considering a bus stop closer to the village if enough children need to go to secondary school in the town.

'Monica has contacted a local nature conservation group about the coppice for me. Apparently, they were delighted, and are happy to sort out the legalities as soon as all the rest is settled.' She paused. 'I'd like you to be part of all this, too, love.'

Catrin didn't feel left out any more. She laughed softly.

'You don't need me. It sounds as

though you have plenty of help already. If you are happy with all the plans and everything else, then that's the main thing. I'll help in any way I can if there is something I can do, but it seems like everything is bowling along smoothly at the moment.'

'It is, and in a way it's exciting. Everything is falling into place, although there is a lot of legal rigmarole to settle before the proper planning starts. It's a good thing, because Alex has more than enough to contend with at present.'

Knowing that he wasn't yet involved with work at the museum, she was puzzled.

'Alex? Is something wrong?'

'Anne was involved in a car accident in Paris on the same day I came out of hospital. She broke a couple of ribs and one arm, had temporary concussion, and a lot of minor cuts and bruises. He sounded worried when he first rang me to tell me he wouldn't be calling for some time, but he was more optimistic when he rang the other day.'

'Is she still in hospital?'

'No, not any more. Once they'd done all the necessary tests and fixed her up, she could go home. Alex persuaded her to go to stay with her parents until everything has healed properly. She didn't want to go at first, because they live on an isolated farm in Provence, but Alex can be very persuasive and told her she'd recover faster if she forgot work for a while and just concentrated on getting better. He even took her there.'

'I imagine that any car accident is nerve-racking, and upsets anyone involved. Last time I was home, David told me about a van that forced its way on to the roundabout near their house, and nearly caused a pile-up. David wasn't even hurt but it shook him up, no end.'

'Road accidents always shake you up, whether it is your fault or not. I haven't driven since your uncle died because it was too expensive to keep the car. I soon got used to using the buses. I know the bus timetable like the back of my hand. I hope you always take care when you flit around in your sardine tin.'

Catrin laughed.

'It is not a sardine tin! Just because it's small doesn't mean that it isn't a good car.'

'Hope to see you soon.'

'Me, too. Take care, Hazel. I'll be in touch again soon. You know where I am if you need help.'

★ ★ ★

The weeks passed and Catrin filled in application forms for a couple of jobs that looked promising.

When she called on Hazel, she could see that Monica and Hazel got on well and Catrin felt relieved to know someone would be keeping an eye on her.

There was no talk of Monica looking for other lodgings, so Catrin assumed that Monica and her daughter would continue to stay at the cottage even after the little girl started in the village school, after the summer holidays.

In September, the special exhibition opened and it looked like it would be a success. There was a surge of visitors for the first couple of days, and a steady stream thereafter. The reviews in relevant newspapers and professional magazines were good.

Catrin felt proud and satisfied when she wandered the rooms and saw how all their planning and discussions had produced an informative and first-class impression of the life and achievements of a people and culture that was long dead.

If Alex visited the museum because of the new wing, she didn't see him. Since their heated conversation in the hospital corridor, there was no reason for them to speak to each other. Catrin couldn't imagine a reason or an opportunity that would change that situation.

She felt wretched whenever she thought about that day, but she was relieved and grateful that he hadn't mentioned it to Hazel.

Catrin acted and behaved in the same way as she ever had when she visited Hazel, and no-one ever mentioned the hospital any more. Alex had clearly never told her that he thought Catrin was responsible for Hazel's hospital stay.

She avoided mentioning Alex's name. Sometimes Hazel looked at her carefully when she talked about Alex, and perhaps wondered why Catrin never commented, but she didn't probe.

Regrets still often invaded Catrin's sleepless nights, and she wondered how long it would take to forget Alex and start making a new life for herself. He had never been hers and she was glad that she managed to hide that from everyone.

She hadn't even admitted to Gloria that she'd fallen in love with Alex. Gloria just believed that she wanted to avoid him because she disliked him. Because of that, she didn't need to explain that her attitude had to do with the fact that he loved someone else.

The weekends were the worst times. She had to fill the hours and even reading was a chore.

Long walks helped, but she had never before felt that the weekends were so empty and awful.

★ ★ ★

One afternoon at work, she came down the corridor and glanced up. Her heart jolted when she recognised Alex coming towards her with Bert at his side. Bert beamed and when they drew alongside, he stopped to chat.

'Afternoon, Catrin!'

Catrin concentrated on Bert.

'Afternoon.' She just nodded in Alex's direction. 'Hello, Alex.'

She thanked heaven that he hadn't been on his own.

He smiled smoothly, not betraying if

he was annoyed or not.

'Hello.'

'Alex is attending a meeting of the trustees to discuss some details about the start of building,' Bert explained. 'Lots to sort out yet.'

'I expect so.' She turned to Alex. 'I hope Anne is much better?'

He regarded her quizzically for a moment.

'Yes, she's fine, thanks. She's improving fast.'

Her hands gripped the folder tighter. She smiled hesitatingly.

'Good.'

He was just as attractive as ever. Nothing had changed. Her longing emerged anew, stronger than ever.

'I just took a look at your exhibition. Very impressive!'

'Thank you.' She hoped her smile was noncommittal.

Bert nodded.

'Yes, it is excellent. Don't want to nag, Alex, but we must push on.'

'Yes, of course.' His voice was

231

neutral. 'Good to see you again, Catrin. We must have a proper chat soon. I've been very busy lately otherwise we might have seen each other before now.'

Her breath caught in her throat and she chose her response carefully.

'Perhaps.'

There was nothing for them to discuss. Another meeting would change nothing and seeing him only caused more heartache. Their only possible link in future would be Hazel.

The two men turned away and Catrin looked stiffly ahead as she covered the rest of the corridor in the opposite direction with determined steps. She detoured to wash her face with cold water on the way, and then continued on her way to deposit the folder with a colleague in one of the other offices.

Back in her own office, she stared unseeingly out of the window at the tops of some trees waving in the gentle winds. The first signs of autumn were biting at the edges of the leaves.

In a couple of weeks, they would be a glorious mixture of reds and gold. She'd miss the trees when she went. They were already old friends.

On her way home, she noticed a group of birds grouped on the electric wires near her flat. She wondered if they were migrating birds, gathering before they left for warmer climes.

When she reached home, there was a letter requesting her to attend an interview for a job she'd applied for near Inverness in Scotland. It was for someone who needed a manager to run a private art gallery, and organise occasional special events and displays.

It sounded just right for her, and at this very moment, it felt almost like a godsend. She would be far, far away from the danger of unforeseen meetings Alex.

She would miss old friends and the ones she'd made at the museum, but her present priority was to get away.

Hazel would continue to inform her of Alex's marriage, his children, his work — and that would be hard enough to bear, but if she changed her work and her surroundings it would cut him out of her life, and she would have a better chance of a new start.

She would never forget him, but she hoped the longings would fade in time.

Shock Announcement

Catrin took a day off to go to the interview. The gallery was the west wing of a sturdy dark grey castle overlooking some breathtaking scenery, including a large dark loch in the bowl of the mountains in the far distance.

It was windy and Catrin pulled her coat tighter around herself as she got out of her car and climbed the steps.

It seemed a lonely place, but the owner was a pleasant man in his fifties. He was slim with pale grey eyes and salt and pepper hair.

He showed her round the gallery before leading her back to the main part of the castle where he and his wife talked to her and offered a cup of welcome tea.

His wife was petite and had bright blue eyes.

'This is a bit off the beaten track for a

young girl from the south. Do you think you'll fit in? There isn't a hive of social activity around here, although the people are very welcoming once they know you.'

'I'll enjoy the change and the challenge. You have some noteworthy items in the gallery, and I think I could increase interest in them. Do you get many visitors?'

'Quite a few in the summer and autumn, but visitors are rare in wintertime,' her husband answered.

Catrin nodded.

'That would give me lots of leeway to try out new ideas to attract more people — as long as I have your approval to do so, of course.'

'One of my forefathers had an urge to collect art. I find that most of what he bought is quite depressing, but I can't ignore it completely, even though it costs the earth to keep the gallery heated properly.'

Catrin smiled warmly and accepted a piece of offered shortbread.

'Oh, it's not all depressing and you have some very interesting pictures. Perhaps I can improve on that interest and bring in more visitors to the gallery and include it as part of a tour of the castle.'

'That would be a godsend.'

'Would you object if I included the work of local art groups and societies now and then? Perhaps I could organise special exhibitions on a particular theme. People and museums are usually quite happy to lend their exhibits for a short time if the pictures are properly insured.

'Some of the rooms are almost bare. It would be easy to use them for those kind of projects.'

'Heavens! You are thinking ahead, aren't you?'

'Well, I wouldn't want to sit around twiddling my thumbs all through the winter if it is a slack time for visitors. I hope that when people get to know me, they'll trust me and lend well-known pieces of art for exhibitions.'

'People are wary, it's part of their character, but once you are accepted they're good sorts. It isn't in your favour that you are a Sassenach, but you can't help that. You are happy with what we're offering — moneywise?'

She nodded. It was far less than she was earning at present, but she wasn't likely to need as much when she lived here.

'Is there somewhere close by where I can rent a flat or a house?'

He scratched his chin.

'You came through the village on the way here. There is bound to be somewhere suitable. People come and go all the time, especially the younger generation.

'I'm glad to say, though, that some of them are beginning to return. The biggest problem is finding work. One or two people have started up their own businesses, and they work online from here now.'

'I love the scenery. I can imagine lots of walks in my leisure time.'

'Yes, we get a lot of visiting ramblers, but you have to be careful, especially in winter. Anyone who sets off and doesn't know exactly where he or she is will end up in trouble if the weather turns bad.'

It sounded daunting, but Catrin decided it would be an interesting challenge if they liked her enough to offer her the job. They chatted for a little longer and when she got up to leave, he smiled warmly.

'We'll be in touch, promise. That will give us, and you, time to think things through carefully.'

As she drove past the cottages of rough stone in the small nearby village, she noticed a small shop-cum-post office, a pub and another building that announced it was the local bank and the library.

A hardware shop was right at the end of the village, next to a building yard. There was no-one in sight anywhere.

She thought about a meal in the pub, but decided against it and pressed on. She had a long journey ahead of her.

* ★ *

Three days later the letter arrived telling her she could have the job if she wanted it. Catrin decided it was fair to warn someone in the museum. She asked Irene if she could talk to Bert for a couple of minutes. Irene waved her through.

His initial smile faded when she explained why she was there.

'But why, Catrin? This is a big surprise. Are you dissatisfied here? Have these people offered you more money?'

'No, I just feel I ought to make a change. I've been here for over five years.'

'And I expected you would be here for five more. We would miss you sorely, Catrin. You've done some sterling work. It isn't easy to imagine anyone else who could do your job as well as you do.'

'That's kind of you to say so, and I have been happy here. You gave me a lot of freedom and you never jumped on my toes. In fact I'll miss everyone.'

'Then why go?'

She felt a lump in her throat.

'I need a change. Personal reasons. I haven't written my acceptance yet but I wanted to warn you in plenty of time.

'I'm almost sure that they won't mind if I come a few weeks later, if you have difficulty finding someone quickly. Apparently there isn't so much activity in this place in winter.'

'Where is it?'

She told him.

'It sounds rather forbidding.'

'The local scenery is wonderful and the owner seems very nice.'

'Well this certainly takes the wind out of my sails. It's so unexpected. I suppose I should wish you luck, but I hope you'll change your mind before you sign anything.'

She got up.

'I won't steal any more of your time. I'm sure that you are busy, but I wanted you to be the first to know.'

He looked at her for a few seconds.

'Yes, I must get on, but I hope we can have a chat about this again before you make your final decision?'

He glanced at the old coaching clock on the wall.

'I'm meeting Alex Lorenzi in a couple of minutes. He promised me a rough timetable on the various stages of work on the new wing.'

Alerted and not wanting to meet him in the corridor, or on the stairs, she stood up hurriedly.

'I'll be in touch and keep you informed, Bert.'

'Yes, you do that, and don't forget that we need to have another chat about all this before you make your final decision.'

Catrin looked at her watch. It was almost time to go home. She took an indirect route to her office through a couple of galleries. Once she was there, she shouldered her bag, and scurried down the back stairs.

She saw Alex's convertible in the parking lot and sighed with relief that she hadn't bumped into him.

Once inside her flat she threw her keys on the hall table, took off her shoes, and unpinned her hair so that it now framed her face. Changing her skirt and blouse for jeans and a T-shirt, she made herself a mug of coffee in her compact kitchen, with its cream tiles and natural wood cupboards, and carried it into the sitting-room.

It was elegant, with clean, uncluttered modern design and she wondered how much of it she could take with her to furnish her new home in Scotland.

When the doorbell rang, she went to open the door, and the breath caught in her throat. Alex was the last person she expected to find on her doorstep.

She lost her voice for a second then pulled herself together.

'What are you doing here? I think we've said all there is to say to each other, or do you have a message from Hazel? I can't think of any other reason.'

Her colour heightened and she

wished he'd go away.

He stood looking uncomfortable.

'Before you slam the door in my face, please give me a chance to clear the air.'

'There's nothing that we need to clear. I know how we stand.' All of a sudden, she wondered how he'd found her. 'How did you know where I live?'

As she waited and looked up at him, the colour receded and returned in force. Confusion filled her being and her thoughts were a complete muddle.

'Can I come in?'

There was no logical reason to refuse him. She wasn't going to be offensive. She stepped aside.

'Yes, of course.'

He was too big for her hallway. He took off his coat and hung it on one of the hooks. She waited and then led the way into her sitting-room.

He followed her with easy strides and ignored her indication that he should sit down.

'Bert told me that you were thinking of leaving the museum,' he stated flatly, 'that you are going to take a job in Scotland?'

His expression was daunting.

'Is that true?'

She nodded and her voice sounded croaky.

'And what has that got to do with you? I didn't think Bert would spread it around so fast. I only forewarned him this afternoon.'

'I don't think he has told anyone yet or that he will, until he has your official notice in his hands. He's not that type of administrator.

'I just asked if you were in and I think he presumed I'd already know all about your plans. It slipped in during his conversation and I asked him for your address. I think he realised then that we weren't as close as he thought we were. He hesitated before he gave it to me, but eventually gave in.'

She was curious and recovered enough to ask.

'I still don't understand why you've gone to the bother of following me home. We didn't part on the best of terms last time, in the hospital. You demonstrated quite clearly what you thought of me.' She bit her lip and waited.

'Simply because I love you, and I don't want you to go to Scotland.'

Once in a Lifetime

The air left Catrin's lungs, and she took a quick breath of utter astonishment.

'Don't be absurd! You don't even like me. Your accusations that day at the hospital told me so. Anyway, you don't love me, you love Anne.' She was clinging to the remnants of common sense.

He looked puzzled.

'Anne? What has Anne got to do with you and me?'

'She's your girlfriend. Everyone assumes so.'

His eyebrows lifted.

'Who is everyone, and why do they assume such rubbish?'

'Hazel does, I do, and the people in the museum that day thought so, too. It was obvious that she is very devoted to you.'

'I hope she is, but in a dedicated,

professional way. Anne is my assistant. A darned good assistant and she's a qualified surveyor. She's been with me for a couple of years. She is also very committed to her boyfriend and they are getting married early next year.'

Catrin could only manage a faint 'Oh.'

Sounding a little impatient, he continued to explain.

'She's engaged to a man who works for the government in Paris. He keeps telling me that it's about time I gave her an office in Paris, or even let her work from home. I'm thinking of doing so. She'd have more time to do what I need her to do, and wouldn't waste her time travelling around just to supply me personally with information. The arrangement of her meeting me to finalise agreements has become an unnecessary habit.

'But . . . never mind about Anne! I don't understand why anyone picked up the wrong impression about us, but it looks like you did, too. You, and everyone else, are wrong.'

'So, you're not . . . '

He shook his head and smiled. Catrin needed a moment to absorb the information. He was free, and it must mean something that he had followed her home this evening.

He bent his head, took her hand, and kissed the back and then turned it to kiss the palm. He held on to it tightly.

Her breath rose and fell faster, and Catrin was sure he must hear the beat of her heart. It was much too loud. Her mouth felt dry and she stared at him, before she recalled his words.

She looked up at him.

'You don't like me, we don't know each other very well, and we've only spent a couple of hours together. You can't possibly love me.'

He considered her with amusement.

'It is possible. I am in love with you. I think I was attracted from the moment I met you. After Corsica, I knew it had to be you, no-one else will ever do. Give me a chance! Give us a chance! I've never met anyone who attracts me in this way before. I've never met anyone who fills my senses, or invades my dreams with so much longing. I understand that you have the right to be mad at me, and I'm praying there is no-one else in your life. I'm hoping you can forgive the way I reacted in the hospital that day.'

She braced herself and she could tell that he was enjoying the sight of her confusion.

'If you like me, you have a strange way of showing it. You were extremely rude and very hurtful that afternoon.'

He ran one hand through his hair before he planted them on either side of her waist.

'Agreed, I was. I was appallingly rude and offensive. My only excuse is that I have a phobia about hospitals and I act irrationally every time I'm in one. I had my appendix out when I was a small kid and it was an old-fashioned place. They were strict about visiting times. I missed my parents and didn't understand what was going on.

'Today, if I get a whiff of disinfectant, the hairs on the back of my neck stand up. That day, you took the brunt of my foul mood. I knew you weren't responsible for Hazel's problems.' He sighed. 'I waited to apologise, but you slipped away before I could. I know very well that I didn't consider the facts, or your point of view. They always say you hurt the one you love, and I did that day.

'I intended to phone and put things right, but then Anne had her accident. Once I settled her at her parents, her work landed on my desk, and began to pile up. When I talked to Bert this afternoon I was shocked to hear you were thinking of leaving.'

Catrin was thinking about him as a frightened little boy, cut off from the people he loved, in a strictly run hospital. She nodded silently. Today he was a figure of authority and a formidable entrepreneur. Despite all her previous misgivings, any remaining resistance began to melt.

She decided that if he did love her it was nothing short of amazing. She took a tentative step forward.

'It's OK about what happened at the hospital. If I'd known about your fears, I'd have understood better. I did mind your hurtful words very much at the time.' She relaxed and laughed. 'What happens if you ever need to go into hospital?'

He looked at her and laughed.

'Goodness only knows! Perhaps I ought to get some therapy in case that happens.'

'I think that is an excellent idea.'

He stared at her for a long, long moment.

'I don't know how you do it, but you bewitch me,' he murmured.

His lips touched hers with a tenderness that was deceiving, and she felt herself dissolving into sheer delight. It looked like he felt the same enchantment and a fierce exhilaration swept through her as his lips became more demanding.

They were together at last. She felt the joy of his hands, and the touch of his lips.

He stroked her hair back off her face.

'Do you love me?' he asked softly.

Without any hesitancy now, she looked up into his dark eyes.

'Yes, I do.'

'I don't deserve you, but I'll do my best to love you all my life.' After another satisfying kiss, his arms cradled her and he rocked her gently. 'When Bert told me that you are thinking of hopping off to Scotland, I couldn't believe that fate was so unkind. You were moving out of my life without knowing how much I love you.' He shifted his hands to her shoulders again.

Catrin smiled sweetly at him. She reached up and kissed him, then spoke quietly.

'I think I'd like us to be together, to be happy together.'

His gaze roved and he appraised her lazily. Her heart jolted and her pulse pounded. He chuckled knowingly and pulled her towards him until his nearness kindled feelings of fire.

This was what she had dreamed of. He was her soulmate, she was sure of that. The pleasure of knowing they belonged, that he wanted them to belong, and that this was just the beginning, allowed contentment and peace to flood through her being.

He kissed the side of her throat.

'What do you think about spending this weekend on Corsica? Just you and me.'

Catrin just felt delight and nodded.

'Can't think of anything I'd like more.'

'And promise me you won't go to Scotland?' he whispered, holding her at arms' length. 'I couldn't bear it if you are that far away. It's already complicated enough to have you here and me in London, Paris, or wherever I happen to be.'

Feeling breathless but more confident now, she slipped her arms around his waist, and looked up into his face. It felt so right.

'I could look for a job in London, if you like.'

He whooped.

'That's a wonderful idea. But as long as I'm working on the new wing, I could stay here with you, couldn't I? When it's finished you could then find a job in London, or wherever I happen to be.'

She gave out a peal of laughter.

'You are a chauvinist! Why should I follow you? You could follow me. Is this just all about you getting lodgings for the duration of the building?'

His eyes twinkled. He picked her up and swung her around.

'No! I don't care where I live as long as I'm with you. It's just my growing longing to be with you as much as I can from now on. Nothing and no-one will pull us apart ever again. You are my twin soul.'

A sudden thought brought Catrin back to earth.

'What will Hazel say?'

'She'll be delighted and happy, but she can never be as happy as I am.' He kissed her again and his eyes filled with unspoken promises. 'Let's be sensible and practical. I'll give you half-an-hour to pack your bag. I'll occupy myself with doing something useful, like watering the plants, doing the washing-up, or darning your socks.'

Catrin tried to look livid.

'I wash up as I go along, and no-one darns anything in this day and age.'

'Then it will have to be the plants! We'll drive up to London and if there's no chance of getting to Corsica this evening, we'll celebrate in London and go first thing tomorrow morning.'

'I have to be back in work on Monday.'

He kissed her forehead.

'So do I, but let's be foolish and just enjoy life for a day or two. The house is the perfect place for us to be on our

256

own. I built it for this moment. Without knowing it, I built it for you. I'd take you there for just one hour if that was all we had. We have to make up for lost time. I love you, Catrin.'

He studied her face held between his hands. She didn't doubt it for a moment.

'I love you very much,' he added. 'I love you more than I ever believed I could love anyone. That will never change. It is my once in a lifetime.'

Catrin considered him for a moment. He was unwavering and impressive. He liked to have everything under control, and he was sometimes proud and too self-sufficient. He was also caring, hardworking, and reliable.

His wicked grin made him her real-life hero, and she loved him more than words could express. She felt excited and happy; so very, very happy.

She'd found her safe haven at last, and the future looked good. The gods had finally decided they belonged together, and now nothing would ever drive them apart again.

IT'S NEVER TOO LATE
THE MOST WONDERFUL TIME
OF THE YEAR
THE SILVER LINING
THE POTTERY PROJECT
SOMETHING'S BREWING
KINDRED HEARTS

We do hope that you have enjoyed reading this large print book.

Did you know that all of our titles are available for purchase?

We publish a wide range of high quality large print books including:
**Romances, Mysteries, Classics
General Fiction
Non Fiction and Westerns**

Special interest titles available in large print are:
**The Little Oxford Dictionary
Music Book, Song Book
Hymn Book, Service Book**

Also available from us courtesy of Oxford University Press:
**Young Readers' Dictionary
(large print edition)
Young Readers' Thesaurus
(large print edition)**

For further information or a free brochure, please contact us at:
**Ulverscroft Large Print Books Ltd.,
The Green, Bradgate Road, Anstey,
Leicester, LE7 7FU, England.
Tel:** (00 44) **0116 236 4325
Fax:** (00 44) **0116 234 0205**

A YEAR IN JAPAN

Patricia Keyson

When ex-librarian Emma announces she's accepted a year-long position to teach English in Japan, the news shocks her grown children. Enjoying single life after half a year of estrangement from her husband Neil, Emma can't wait to embark upon her adventure in three weeks. Then Neil is hospitalised after a car accident, and needs a carer at home while he recovers. Emma is the only one available to help. Three weeks — can Neil make up for lost time before Emma leaves, and will she let him back into her heart?

GRANDPA'S WISH

Sarah Swatridge

Melanie is growing tired of her job at a family law firm, until she is tasked with tracing a Mr Davies, the beneficiary of a late client's estate. Tracking him down, Melanie is surprised to find Robbie-Joe uninterested in the terms of the will, especially when he learns that it belonged to a grandfather he had no idea existed. To claim his fortune, Robbie-Joe must complete twelve challenges in twelve months. But Melanie has a challenge of her own: to stop her feelings for Robbie-Joe becoming anything more than professional . . .

HOME TO MISTY MOUNTAIN

Jilly Barry

UK-born Hayley Collins is visiting Australia, staying with a friend and looking for work. Craig Maxwell runs a holiday resort at Misty Mountain, a four-hour drive from Melbourne. When Hayley applies to be an administrator at the resort, Craig takes her on — and much else besides. She has to return to England in twelve months. He's engaged to a woman whose father is helping to keep the resort's finances in the black. so when Hayley and Craig fall in love, it seems a future together is only a distant dream . . .

RUBY LOVES . . .

Christina Garbutt

Crime writer Adam finds the peace he needs to finish his latest novel in a remote stately home in Carwyn Bay, Wales — at least until effervescent, disaster-prone Ruby arrives to run the tourist café while also pursuing a secret plan to uncover her grandfather's past. Through baking disasters and shocking revelations, they find themselves falling in love. But Ruby is saddened by what she learns about her grandfather, and plans to go home to America at the end of the summer. Will their relationship be strong enough to last?

ROMANCE AT THE CAT CAFÉ

Suzanne Ross Jones

Maxine Flynn leaves behind her unful-filling accountancy job and unsupportive fiancé to live her dream of owning a cat café. Her beloved cats keep her company, so there's no room for romance — until she meets hand-some next-door grocer Angus McRae, who conceals a warm heart under a gruff exterior. But with the grocery losing money and customers, and Maxine dealing with an unwelcome visitor from her past, plus mischie-vous lost cats, the road to romance isn't always a smooth one. Will they be able to make a future together?

A FAIR EXCHANGE

Susan Udy

Tara Wyndham has a busy life: she manages a beauty salon, That Special Touch, as well as the five-year-old daughter of her ne'er-do-well young brother and single father, Ricky. Things get complicated when Ricky vanishes without a trace, and Tara is apprised of an impending visit from Gray Madison, owner of the business which has recently taken over her salon. And he has a reputation for being utterly ruthless. So why does Tara find herself feeling attracted to him — and what is she to do about Ricky?